CARJACKED

SELENA WINTERS

CONTENTS

PLAYLIST

"Sweater Weather"— The Neighbourhood
"Prisoner"—Miley Cyrus feat Dua Lipa
"Dark Paradise"—Lana Del Rey
"Animal"— Troye Sivan
"Elastic Heart"—Sia
"Closer"—Nine Inch Nails
"My strange addiction"—Billie Eilish
"Blinding Lights"—Weeknd
"Heathens" — Twenty One Pilots

You can find the playlist on Spotify here

AUTHOR'S NOTE

*H*ello readers,

This story explores dark romance and contains explicit content that may not be suitable for all readers. It includes themes of dominance, psychotic behavior, possessiveness, and explicit mature scenes presented alongside delicate subject matters that may be distressing or triggering for some individuals.

Please refer to this comprehensive <u>list</u> of warnings on my website for detailed information on potential triggers.

I advise reader discretion and recommend only proceeding if you're comfortable with the mentioned themes. Rest assured, the story ends in a HEA with no cliffhanger or cheating between the main characters.

DEDICATION

To all the girls who think a huge, tattooed psychopath with a pierced cock will fuck like a beast, let me tell you, you're absolutely right. Enjoy...

1

LILA

Speeding away from my boyfriend's home, I'm so angry I could kill him. He knows how important my parent's party is tonight, but he's too busy going out, getting drunk, and watching the game. It's embarrassing. I should walk out on him and never look back, but he's an asshole who's got a lot of influence in Illinois.

He threatens to ruin my journalism career whenever I say I'm leaving him. A part of me wonders if that would be a good thing since I'd love to pursue my blogging career full-time, but I know he'd probably find a way to destroy that, too. The annoying thing is, he's got the power to do so. Which means I'm stuck in a never-ending cycle of disappointment and dissatisfaction with a man who refuses to let me go. He uses my career to blackmail me, and I'm fucking fed up with it. There's got to be a way out.

He's a powerful and influential politician and his Daddy owns half of Illinois. I'm not sure what I was thinking dating a politician and rich boy like him. I've got no idea how I'd evade him other than leaving the state, which would mean leaving my parents. Unless I can find some dirt to use against him, but he's so fucking secretive all the time.

Tonight is my mom and dad's thirtieth wedding anniversary party. And I've got to turn up there alone and make excuses for why Brian isn't attending. I hate him so much.

The tires of my worn-out car pound against the tarmac as I race down the road away from Chicago toward Clarendon Hills, where my parents live. Tonight is supposed to be a joyful celebration. Instead, I feel angry and hopeless.

There's a sudden pop followed by the grating of a flat tire rubbing against the tarmac, making panic twist like a cobra in my gut. Just my fucking luck. I pull over onto the side of the highway and switch on my hazards.

"You've got to be fucking kidding me." I get out of the car and scream in frustration. When I pop open the trunk of the car, my heart sinks. That's when I remember Brian took the jack for his car because he's too much of a douchebag to go and buy his own despite having more than enough money. There's no way I can change this tire without it. Tears fill my eyes, but I don't allow them to fall.

What's the point?

I pull out my cell phone, and when I see I've got no service, I'm sure forces are working against me. I'm not even that far out of the city. There should be cell service, for fuck's sake.

The surrounding forest appears menacing, its gnarled branches reaching out with wicked claw-like fingers. Desperation washes over me like a cold, suffocating wave.

How can this night get any worse?

Just as I'm about to break down, I notice a figure in the distance approaching me. A tall and broad-shouldered man with a rough exterior that could scare off anyone from a mile away. His intimidating presence, with his face obscured by a hood and hands covered in tattoos, only adds to my fear. His intense gaze pierces through the darkness, sending a shiver cascading down my spine. I contemplate jumping into the car and locking the door, but he's the only person I can ask for help.

When he notices my flat tire, he slows and approaches me. A heavy scent of musk and tobacco waft toward me, mingling with the crisp night air. The closer he gets, the more I realize despite his roughness, he's ridiculously handsome with thick, dark, medium-length hair and dark brown eyes that seem to reflect the dim street lights. His jaw is strong, and if I didn't know any better, I'd say he looks like a male model. And he has to be about six foot four tall. But there's too much of a dangerous aura around him for that to be his profession.

I sense this is the kind of man you should run from, not ask for help.

"Need a hand?" he asks.

"I, uh, blew a tire," I stammer. "I've got a spare, but no jack and…"

Without hesitation, he steps closer. "Don't worry, I'll change it." He goes to the side of the road and picks up an old discarded metal pole that looks like it was once a traffic sign. "Just need some leverage." He grabs a huge rock, and then I watch as he uses the two objects instead of a jack, managing to get the tire off the ground enough to change it.

He reaches for the tools in the trunk of my car. Though marked with the ink of countless tattoos, his hands move with surprising gentleness and agility as he changes the tire. The silence between us is deafening until he finally breaks it.

"You should check your tires often. You're lucky I was passing by."

"You're telling me," I reply, giving him a feeble smile. "Thanks for your help."

He nods, "Just doing what anyone should." He finishes tightening the last bolt and stands up, dusting his hands. And then he releases the makeshift jack, tossing it aside. "Where's a woman like you going all alone dressed like that?" His eyes move down the length of my body, making goosebumps rise over every inch of my skin.

I swallow hard as his gaze is nothing short of preda-tory. "A party. I'm late, and my parents will wonder where I am." I give him a forced smile. "Thanks for your help, but I need to get going—"

He grabs my wrist, stopping me in my tracks. "You're not going anywhere." He meets my gaze, and his eyes darken. "You shouldn't be out here traveling alone and let a man like me help," he says.

I swallow hard. "Why not?"

He smirks, sending a shiver down my spine. And then the atmosphere shifts as he pulls a gun from his hoodie, making my heart freeze in my chest.

"Get in the car and drive," he orders, pointing the gun at me.

His command echoes in my ears, jarring me to the core. For a moment, I falter, my mind whirling with possibilities. Could I scream for help or attempt to run for it? I quickly dismiss the idea; we're on a back road and not close to any houses, with no one around to hear me. I curse myself then for taking the back roads to avoid traffic as if this had happened on the main roads, I'd be fine. I glance at the gun, its metallic gleam cold and threatening in his hand, and realize that arguing or running isn't an option.

My stomach churns with fear. The gravity of the situation settles in, making my legs buckle. My throat suddenly dry, and my heart is pounding like a jackhammer as I take a deep breath and step toward the car. My hands shake as I reach for the door.

The cool leather makes me shiver as I slide into the driver's seat, placing my trembling hands on the steering wheel and feeling the familiar texture beneath my fingertips.

I glance at the tattooed man as he gets in beside me, still aiming the gun at me. The engine's roar breaks the stifling silence.

I swallow hard, my heart pounding like a drum against my ribcage. With one last glance at the man beside me, I grip the steering wheel tightly, put the car into drive, and press down on the accelerator. "Where am I driving?"

"No questions, just stay on this road."

I nod, my jaw clenched as I focus on the road ahead. My mind races, trying to devise a plan of escape while also keeping an eye out for any opportunity. But every time I think of something, I remember the gun and the cold, calculating look in this man's eyes.

After about ten minutes, he reaches for my purse on the floor, making me tense. And then he pulls out my cell phone and chucks it out of the window, making my stomach drop. The one thing that could have been used to track me is gone. I almost release a sob but hold it back. I don't want him to think I'm weak.

As we drive for what feels like hours, I try to keep track of our location, but soon realize we're deep into the countryside with no recognizable landmarks. Panic sets in as I realize how helpless I am.

My night, which was horrible before, has now turned into a nightmare.

Is there a way out of this?

I've got no idea, but I know I have to try.

One thing at a time, Lila, I tell myself. *First, get through this night. Then, think about how to escape.* I take a deep breath, gripping the steering wheel tighter as I continue to drive into the unknown, feeling vastly underprepared for what comes next.

2
ASH

The moonlight dances across her face, illuminating her features and making her look celestial. Damn, she's beautiful. The kind of woman who makes a man's blood pump harder and faster. Right now, all I can think about is the searing need coursing through my veins. It's been too long. My gaze is glued to her, watching every nervous twitch and panicked glance she throws my way. It amuses me.

Her palpable fear fills the car with a heady tension that thrills me. There's something about it, the raw, primal fear that screams survival. It's intoxicating. And it's all because of me. I'm the predator here, the omnipotent force driving her into a frenzy of fear as we tear down this desolate road.

I study her; her hands are tight around the steering wheel until her knuckles turn bone-white, and her heart beats so frantically in her neck, like a bird trapped in a cage. She's an interesting puzzle, this one, and I can't wait to solve it.

Her attempts to remain calm and her struggle to keep her wits about her only fuel my desire more.

This is power, the kind of power I've been starving for inside. The kind of power that makes my heart pound with anticipation. This is the fear I can taste, the control I can manipulate, and the thrill I can hardly wait for. And this beautiful, terrified woman is the catalyst to it all.

I lean back in my seat, a smirk playing on my lips as I watch her wrestle with her emotions. It's been a while since I've been this entertained. Her terror is my ecstasy. Her dread is my delight. After years in prison, this is exactly what I need.

And I want her. God help me. I want her. But for now, I can wait. I've got all the time in the world. First, I need to get far away from this state. Pulling the pack of cigarettes and lighter that I stole from a security guard out of my jacket, I light one up.

She clears her throat. "Do you mind? I don't want my car stinking of smoke."

I smirk as she tries to sound brave. "I don't give a shit. I need a smoke." Drawing a deep inhale, I roll the window and blow it out of the car. "I'll blow the smoke out the window." Instantly, it calms me and the ravenous hunger grating at my insides. My cock has been hard since I set eyes on her.

Her jaw clenches, and she tightens her grip on the

steering wheel to contain her anger. Maybe she's not as scared as I first thought.

"Where are we going?" she asks again.

It's been a couple of hours since I got in her car, so her restraint is admirable not to have spoken for this long. I can detect a slight tremor in her voice, indicating she's still scared.

I remain silent for a moment, savoring the tension. Then, without shifting my gaze from the road ahead, I say, "Far away from this state."

My response only serves to heighten her fear, but somehow, she finds a drop of courage to nod, and we continue our journey enveloped in heavy silence.

After another hour, I spot a seedy motel on the road just over the Illinois border. "Stop here," I demand.

Without hesitation, she pulls the car into the motel's parking lot. "Turn off the engine," I order. She does as told, turning the key and glancing fearfully at me. "And now," I say, my voice low and steady, "You're going to go in there and get us a room." I pull out some cash I stole from the security guard and pass it to her. "And if you even think about messing with me..." I let my words hang in the air for a moment. I don't need to finish the sentence. The implication is clear.

She nods before getting out of the car.

I watch her go, a dangerous mix of lust and power pumping through my veins.

As she walks toward the office, I let my eyes trail her, lost in the curve of her hips and the sway of her ass. The tightness in my jeans becomes unbearable, an acute reminder of the years I've spent deprived of such a sight.

I shift in my seat, my hand dropping to my lap. Slipping it beneath the waistband of my jeans, my fingers trace the outline of my hard dick. The pressure of the fabric against my piercings sends a jolt of pleasure through my body, intensifying the throbbing ache that's been torturing me for the past few hours. As I watch her move further away, the cold metal of the prince Albert piercing rubbing against the rough denim fabric heightens my pleasure.

My breaths turn ragged as the imagined fantasy in my mind grows vivid.

The thrill of being the predator, stalking my prey makes me harder than nails. Unable to contain myself any longer, I unbutton my jeans, my hand delving into my briefs. The moment my fingers wrap around my cock, a low moan escapes my lips.

I stroke myself, slowly at first, lost in the mix of relief and anticipation.

Each touch sends a sharp, tantalizing sensation through the piercings, rubbing the cold metal with each stroke.

As I sit alone in her car, my mind wanders into the dark corners of my psyche, painting vivid fantasies of her. I imagine her pinned beneath me, those beautiful eyes wide with fear and something akin to desire. Even while she screams at me to stop, her pussy is dripping wet and hungry for my dick.

As I stroke myself, each tug brings me closer to the edge. My mind fills with images of her curves, fear, and defiance. And it's the thought of her that fuels my desire.

And then the sound of the car door opening jolts me back to reality, my hand freezing in its rhythm. In the dim glow of the dashboard lights, her face whitens as her eyes flick to my hard cock.

She gasps, a strangled sound trapped between surprise and fear.

"Get in," I demand.

She does as she's told, sitting behind the wheel.

A smirk creeps onto my face as I take in her reaction. "Like what you see, sweetheart?" I shoot her a heated glance, my voice dripping with raw desire. "Don't act so innocent. I can see that glint in your eyes. It's not just fear, is it? You're curious. You're intrigued."

Her voice is shaky. "You're insane." Even as she tells me that, I can see the lie in her eyes. And as she glances down at my cock again, her thighs clench together.

My dirty starlight.

That's what she is.

The light to my dark.

The balm to my wounds.

"Do you mind if I finish?" I ask her, my voice strained with pent-up desire. "It's been a long time since I've had such exquisite inspiration for my fantasies." I allow my eyes to rove over her, devouring her with them.

I watch as she swallows hard.

Her cheeks are red as she watches me stroke my cock,

unashamedly enjoying the show I'm giving her. And then I notice her thighs start to move.

Dirty girl.

My voice drops to a husky whisper as I share the dark desires flooding my mind. "You know, I've got this fantasy." I gaze down at my stiff cock, then let my eyes slowly travel back to her flushed face. "I see you beneath me, screaming. Begging. Telling me to stop." A wicked grin splits my face at her wide-eyed look. "Your pleas would only encourage me to fuck you harder. I'd love to feel your soft, tight body writhing beneath me while I fill you with my cock." The words hang heavy between us, both a threat and a promise.

Her cheeks flush an even deeper red, and I can see the conflicting emotions dancing in her eyes. Fear and curiosity. Denial and intrigue. I watch her, the smirk never leaving my face.

My body tenses, a low growl rumbling from my chest as I release all over her dashboard, coating it in cum. My chest heaves as I ride out the waves of pleasure, my eyes fixed on hers. And she licks her lips, looking like she wouldn't mind tasting my cum.

"Would you like to clean my dick, baby?"

She shakes her head, nostrils flaring. "No thanks."

I ignore her and grab the back of her head, forcing her lips to my dick. "Suck it clean."

I'm not a good person. Hell, I'm the worst possible man she could have met tonight.

The girl, whose name I've yet to learn, opens her lips

and sucks on it with more eagerness than I expect. A soft, throaty moan comes from her as she tastes me.

A low growl escapes me as her tongue flicks the tip, lapping up the remnants of my cum from my cock and piercings. "You like that, don't you?" I murmur, my voice husky with need, "Tasting me on your tongue." My fingers entwine in her hair, holding her in place as she continues her ministrations. "Fuck, that feels good," I groan, watching as she swallows around me.

Her eyes flicker to mine, full of innocence and mischief that has me hard again in seconds. "Yeah, baby," I breathe out, "suck me clean."

The taste of me on her tongue ignites something within her, her cheeks flushing a darker hue as she lets out another soft moan.

I can't help but chuckle at her response. A sweet girl like her shouldn't enjoy the taste of a hardened criminal. Yet, here she is, cleaning my cock like a dirty cum slut. I use her hair to pull her mouth off me. And then I kiss her lips roughly and passionately, letting my tongue taste her and my own cum.

"Let's go," I command, shoving my cock back into my pants.

The flicker of shame in her eyes is delicious.

Stepping out of the car, I wait for her to join me, and then I pull her along by her wrist, finding sick pleasure in the shocked gasp that leaves her lips. The night air is cold, but the heat radiating from her body is all the warmth I need. I can still taste her on my tongue, an intoxicating blend of sweetness and sin that has me hooked. I glance at her, watching her teeth sink into her bottom lip.

We enter the room, and the door slams shut behind us.

The girl gazes around the room, an apprehension creeping into her eyes as she takes in the shoddy decor and stained bedding. Her nose turns up a little and she scowls. I can't help but smirk at her reaction.

With a swift tug, I pull her into me. "What's your name?" I demand. The intimacy of the question, juxtaposed with the raw lust in my gaze, only serves to heighten the tension between us. And despite the fear in her eyes, I see a flicker of defiance burning bright.

"I won't ask again, starlight."

Her brow furrows at the nickname. "Lila."

"Lila," I repeat, drawing out the syllables, letting her name roll off my tongue like a prayer. "Beautiful name for a beautiful girl." I take a step closer, backing her against the wall. My fingers trace over her delicate features, the curve of her cheek, the swell of her lips.

I can feel her trembling under my touch, but she doesn't pull away. Her wide eyes stay locked on mine, a silent plea for something I can't quite decipher.

"Hmm, Lila," I mutter, bending down to nuzzle against her throat.

I hear her gasp as my lips touch her skin. The smell of sweet and fresh roses fills my senses, making my head spin. I haven't been with a woman for a long time, not since before being arrested five years ago. But now, her soft body is pressed against me, her heat seeping through the fabric of my clothes, and a primal part of me roars in triumph.

I pull back, looking at her flushed face and her parted lips. The fear is still there in her eyes, but so is curiosity, and beneath it, a spark of desire that matches my own.

"Are you scared, Lila?" I ask, my tone deceptively soft.

She nods in reply.

"That's good," I say, my voice dropping an octave. "Your fear is intoxicating." I step closer, our bodies nearly melding together, eliminating any distance between us. Her breath hitches in her throat, and her pulse quickens. "It's like a drug, pulling me closer, making me want you more."

Her eyes widen, the blue of her irises shrinking as her pupils dilate. I can see her chest rising and falling rapidly and hear the soft whimpers escaping her lips. It's a response that fuels the beast within, which has been starved of a taste of fear, desire, and her.

"Get some sleep," I demand, wanting to ride this wave a little longer and build the tension before I take what I want from her.

My main aim may be to get far away from Illinois, but I can have some fun with her at the same time.

"I need to use the bathroom," she mutters.

I nod to the door on the right. "Have at it."

She rushes into the bathroom and shuts the door, locking it.

I allow her privacy. All the windows in the bathrooms are barred, so there's no way she's escaping.

I strip to my briefs and lie on the bed closest to the door, resting my hands behind my head.

My starlight is trapped with a monster, deliciously unaware of how much she's already become a part of me. This prison break is going to be more entertaining than I ever imagined.

3

LILA

I need to escape.

As I stare at myself in the mirror, I know I've got no idea how. The man who has effectively kidnapped me is insane.

I can still taste his cum in my mouth. He's sick. Fucked in the head. And a part of me fears I am, too. Because when he forced me to wrap my lips around him and suck him clean, I enjoyed it. Hell, I felt a bolt between my thighs the moment I set eyes on his huge, thick pierced cock.

I've never seen a pierced cock before, but it was oddly arousing. I'm still tingling with need right now despite the fact the guy I'm with is mentally unstable and could kill me at any moment. Not to mention, I've got a boyfriend at home, even if he's a complete and utter asshole.

I go to the window, my heart pounding with a desperate glimmer of hope. My fingers tremble as I reach for the latch, pulling it open with a soft creak. But what awaits me on the other side shatters my fleeting hope into a million pieces, thick iron bars, cold and unforgiving under my touch. I let out a shaky breath and close it, before resting my forehead against the cold glass as I assess my prison. My thoughts race alongside my heartbeat.

There's no way out from here, no secret hatch or overlooked exit. I'm trapped. And worse, I have to walk right back to him.

I open the bathroom door slowly, nerves coiling tight in my stomach. He's sprawled out on one of the beds, tattooed arms folded behind his head, his chest rising and falling steadily.

He's asleep. I take a moment, studying him. Dangerous, intoxicating, a walking contradiction. His muscular physique is undeniably attractive, covered in intricate tattoos that beg exploration.

He's everything my boyfriend isn't. He's all man. A criminal, yes, but somehow brimming with an unexpected allure. His dark eyes, now closed, had struck me like a bolt of lightning when we first met. And the hair, thick and medium length, begging for me to run my fingers through.

I shake the thoughts away, berating myself. I can't afford to be distracted.

"Like what you see, starlight?" he asks. One eye-opening and fixing on me.

His voice startles me, a husky tone laced with amusement and something more profound. I stiffen, caught off guard. "I...I was just...," I stutter, unable to form a coherent sentence.

He chuckles, his gaze twinkling with amusement. "Relax, starlight," he says, shifting on the bed and running a hand through his thick hair. "You can share with me if you'd like."

My heart skips a beat, and I can't help but notice how his tattooed muscles flex under the dim light. "No thanks." I rush toward the other bed, still fully dressed, about to get in.

"Not like that," he says.

I freeze and glance at him. "What?"

"Strip. You can't sleep in that dress."

A blush creeps up my cheeks, and my throat goes dry. "I...I can't," I manage to mutter, my voice barely above a whisper.

He raises an eyebrow, his gaze never leaving me. "You'll ruin the dress," he states, his voice thick with that undeniable undercurrent of command. His eyes close as if he's already dismissed the conversation.

I stand there, frozen momentarily, torn between indignation and a strange desire to comply. I take a deep breath, averting my eyes from him.

A knot forms in my stomach as I realize I might have

been drawn toward him under different circumstances. But I push that thought away, reminding myself of my situation.

With a trembling hand, I reach for the zipper of my dress, pulling it down slowly. My cheeks burn with embarrassment, and I'm acutely aware of his presence behind me. I slip out of the dress, my skin prickling with a chill that has nothing to do with the temperature. I hastily grab the covers and slide under them, my back facing him.

I close my eyes, willing my heartbeat to slow. But the fabric of the bedding is cool and crisp, a stark contrast to the heat of my skin. I squeeze my eyes shut, desperate to ignore the pull I feel toward him, the curiosity, the desire. It's wrong, it's dangerous. But it's real and there, gnawing at the edge of my consciousness.

I force myself to breathe, focusing on my chest's rhythmic rise and fall. I have to be strong.

I'm in danger, and I need to find a way out. He destroyed my phone, and if I don't turn up tonight at my parent's party, they'll be worried about me. With any luck, they'll speak to the waste of space that is Brian, and he'll tell them I was on my way. And they'll call the police.

All I can do is try to survive and navigate this twisted situation I've found myself in. It's a terrifying reality, but it's my reality. And for now, there's no escape. I didn't miss the fact that he opted for the bed closest to the door.

Allowing him to fall asleep and sneaking out in a few

hours is tempting. I'd get in my car, drive far, find a pay phone, and reveal his location and what happened to the police. It's the best plan I can come up with right now. I can't pin all my hopes on my parents alerting the police, but I fear escape won't be so easy.

4

LILA

The motel room is swaddled in an eerie silence, broken only sporadically by the hum of the air conditioner and the murmur of voices from the parking lot. I lie on the bed, my eyes wide open, staring at the shadowy ceiling. The glow of the lights outside sneaks through the worn-out curtain, painting an uncanny glow on the peeling wallpaper. The room is a ghostly and grim reminder of where I am and who's with me.

My muscles are tense, and my heart is pounding in my chest, each beat echoing with the deafening reminder of the danger I'm in.

It's as if my kidnapper's presence alone is enough to fill the room with dread. I swallow hard, every swallow echoing like a thunderclap in the silent room.

And then I make my decision. I need to get out of here. With one last glance at the man on the other bed, I slowly, carefully edge out from under the covers. I wince as the springs squeak under my weight, hoping it doesn't wake him. And then I swiftly pull my dress over my head, not bothering to zip it up and slip into my pumps. Before creeping toward the door, feeling my heart hammer in my chest like a drum.

Every second is like an eternity, the distance to the door stretching like a desert. I pray silently to every god I know, begging them to keep him asleep and let me escape.

And then, finally, I'm at the door. I ease it open, making the hinges creak. I glance over my shoulder, praying he's still asleep.

His chest rises and falls evenly, the rhythm lulling in its deceptive serenity. In the dimly lit room, shadows dance across his face, masking the predatory glint I know resides in his eyes. Right now, he looks almost beautiful. A fallen angel, perhaps, with an allure that's as captivating as terrifying. But I know better. A monster lurks beneath the façade. The danger he poses is real, and it's urgent. With a shuddering breath, I turn away and focus on the task before me.

Escape.

The cold night air hits me like a wave as I step outside, the dim glow of the parking lot lights providing little comfort. My heart pounds like a war drum as I move hastily across the asphalt.

A cool gust of wind whips past, making me flinch and quicken my pace. My car is in sight now, a beacon of hope in the darkness. I fumble with my keys, their metallic coldness biting into my palm. As I reach the driver's side door, I risk another glance back toward the motel room, my breath hitching. And then my heart sinks.

The lights are on in the room, which means he's awake. Panic courses through me as I struggle to unlock the car door and slide into it.

In my haste, my keys clatter onto the floor of the car. I scramble to pick them up, my trembling hands making the task far more difficult than it should be. The cold hardness of the keys finds their way back into my grip, and I jam them into the ignition.

For a moment, nothing happens, my heart hammering against my ribcage in the deafening silence. Then, with a roar that cuts through the tension like a knife, the engine comes to life, sending a wave of relief washing over me.

But my moment of comfort is short-lived. Before I can even think about driving away, the passenger side door creaks open, then slams shut with a jarring thud. I don't need to look to know who occupies the seat next to me. His eyes are on me. His gaze is as cold and sharp as the knife he presses against my throat.

"Going somewhere?" His voice slithers through the tense silence. The cold steel of the knife presses harder against my skin. A twisted smile plays on his lips as he revels in the terror that must be evident on my face. "You didn't think I'd let you leave so easily, did you?" His laughter fills the car, chilling me to the bone.

Suddenly, the pressure against my throat intensifies, the thin line of cold steel cutting into my skin. A sharp gasp escapes my lips.

His eyes flicker to the red droplet trickling down my neck, satisfaction gleaming in his dark gaze. "I wonder," he muses, his voice cruelly soft, "how far you'll go to survive?" The knife digs deeper, a silent threat.

My heart pounds louder. Each beat is a countdown to a fate I can't bear to consider. Fear engulfs me, but the anticipation and waiting are far worse.

His laughter rings in my ears. "Let's find out, shall we?" His words echo in the claustrophobic space of the car. "Put your hand under your dress and play with yourself for me."

"W-What?" I stammer.

He presses the knife even harder, making me squeal. "You heard me. Do as you're told."

I gulp, the fear elevating. The cold steel bites into my skin, a constant reminder of my mortality. "Do it."

My heart pounds in my chest, the adrenaline surging through my veins, making my hands shake as I hesitantly comply. I slide my hand under my dress, the fabric rough against my trembling fingers. The touch sends a jolt through me, and I gasp, my body betraying my mind. Underneath the fear and loathing, there's a spark of something unexpected.

Lust.

I hate myself for it, but I can't deny the evidence of my pussy slick with arousal.

I crave more while he watches me. The pressure intensifies, and I bite my lip, stifling a moan.

"That's it, Lila," he drawls, his words a seductive poison. "Fuck yourself with your fingers. Nice and slow." His words weave a spell over me, and I cannot resist.

The cold metal of the knife presses closer to my throat, a chilling reminder of the thin line I'm treading between life and death. "Deeper," he commands. "I want to hear you moan, starlight."

The degradation of the situation is eclipsed by the primal need taking hold of my senses.

I curl my fingers, following his sinister instructions. A moan escapes my lips, more animalistic than human, as I plunge my fingers deep.

His grin widens and the thrill of domination is painted clear across his beautiful features.

His eyes are on me, but his hand moves to his lap, unzipping his trousers with a sound that echoes in the silent car. My eyes widen as he releases his cock. The sight of it hard and dripping precum makes me ache.

"Not so fast, Lila," he murmurs. "Slow down and watch." He strokes himself, his movements slow and deliberate. The image is hypnotizing. I watch, transfixed by his huge, hard pierced dick.

"Imagine your fingers are my cock inside you," he commands. "Stretching you, filling you. Can you feel it?"

His words are a toxic cocktail. The darkness in his eyes mirrors the darkness that's consuming me.

His hand moves faster, the rhythm matching the rhythm of my fingers. The wet sounds of my fingers plunging into my soaking wet pussy fill the car. "You like that, don't you, baby?" he taunts, his voice ragged with lust. "You're aching for me, for my cock. Say it."

His other hand, which until now had remained idle, suddenly springs to action. The cold, sharp edge of the knife presses harder against my throat, cutting deeper.

A small gasp escapes my lips. A mixture of fear and a perverse desire thrives on the pain, heightening my arousal. Yet, as much as his words stir a twisted desire, I refuse to give in. I meet his gaze, silently defying his demand.

"I don't need your confession," he declares. "You don't have to tell me how deep your longing runs. You don't have to, because I know. I can see the raw need in your eyes, how you look at me, and how your body responds." He takes a deep breath. "You'll come for me. Soon enough, you will."

His words hang heavy in the air, the thread of inevitability woven through them. The knife at my throat lifts, and he leans back in the seat.

As if to confirm the insanity that lurks in his eyes, he brings the knife to his lips, licking the small trace of my blood from the blade. It's a sight so unnerving, yet perversely seductive that I find myself on the brink of climax.

The sight of my blood on his tongue, the raw danger he poses — it's all too much. An orgasm rips through me, waves of pleasure crashing in response to the fear-induced adrenaline.

"Good girl," he murmurs, a sickeningly sweet note of approval in his voice. "You come so beautifully for me."

He laces his fingers in my hair, strong and unyielding, as he forces my head to his lap. "Drink me. Take every last drop," he commands, his tone brooking no argument.

There's no time to think, protest, or gather my wits. His cock is thrust into my mouth, filling my throat. The twisted pleasure returns, my body involuntarily responding to his dominance.

And then he's climaxing, a rush of warmth flooding my mouth and sliding down my throat. A moan escapes me, a sound of surrender that echoes in the quiet car, cementing the reality— there's no escape from him, and a small, perverted part of me doesn't want to escape.

5

ASH

The engine's rumble is steady as we take the deserted country roads. Roads that will take us at least double the time to our destination but are essential. There will be a manhunt for me in these parts. I'm not sure I can disappear in Montana, even though my cabin is in the woods in the middle of nowhere.

It's why I need the woman beside me. Lila is my cover. The perfect little pet.

The cool wind rushes through the cracked window, stirring documents on the dashboard. I glance at Lila, her face pale in the glow of the passing street lights. A small town sign whizzes by, barely legible in the dim light.

Still a long way from my cabin in Montana.

I pull a cigarette out of the top pocket of my jacket and pop it in my mouth before sparking it up, using my knees to keep the steering wheel straight. Once it's lit, I take a slow drag, trying to rid my mind of all the dark and dirty thoughts involving my starlight.

I glance over at her, noticing her breathing is shallow. Sleep finally claimed her after I took over driving, and I can't blame her for succumbing. The last fifteen hours have been a whirlwind.

She's a necessity, a tool in my hand. I glance at her again, watching her chest rise and fall. Innocent, fragile, like a bird with a broken wing.

A smirk finds its way onto my face as I observe her, blowing smoke out into her precious car. My heart has no regret or remorse for dragging her into this mess. She's a part of this now — my sick, twisted game.

The sound of her shallow breaths is an intoxicating melody that fills the silent car, fuelling the pit of darkness within me. I'm a predator, and she's my prey. It's twisted. It's wrong. But it's necessary. She's my ticket out, my escape.

Cops are less likely to hassle a couple. If anyone sees us, they'll see a man and his sleeping girlfriend on a late-night drive. Not a fugitive. Not a girl held against her will. I'll keep her close until I've safely reached my cabin, my fortress in the heart of nowhere.

And then? I'll figure it out. But for now, she's my alibi, my shield. The car's fuel gauge catches my eye. It's dipping dangerously close to empty, a blinking warning sign in the otherwise dimly lit dashboard.

Spotting a 24-hour gas station ahead, I ease the car into the deserted forecourt. The station is illuminated by harsh, white fluorescent lights casting long, dark shadows. It's eerily quiet, starkly contrasting the chaos brewing behind the scenes as law enforcement hunts for me.

I can't risk using her credit card, so I pull crumpled bills from my pocket. "Stay put," I whisper to her sleeping form before stepping out into the cold night. I lock the doors to be sure she can't escape and stub out my cigarette on the car before tossing it aside.

I fill the fuel tank and head toward the gas station's convenience store, a glowing beacon in the desolate night. Artificial light spills from its windows, casting an eerie glow on the otherwise dark surroundings.

As I walk in, the chime above the door jingles, announcing my presence. The shop is empty, except for the bored-looking cashier behind the counter, engrossed in a magazine. I grab some energy drinks and snacks — junk food to keep me awake on the long drive ahead.

I avoid eye contact with the cashier when paying for the gas and purchases. As I turn to leave, he gasps. I glance back at him to find his eyes wide and face pale as he stares at something behind me. I whip around, expecting the worst.

There's a TV mounted on the wall behind me with the news channel playing silently. My mugshot fills the screen, listed beneath as 'WANTED.'

For a moment, I consider playing dumb. But as I meet the cashier's shocked gaze in the reflection of the television screen, I know there's no point in pretending. The jig is up.

I launch over the counter at him.

He hardly puts up a fight as I punch him hard in the face, knocking him out. Once he's on the ground, I find something to tie him up with. "Sorry, man, but I've got to get away before you ring the police."

I check his pulse, ensuring he's only unconscious, not dead. It's a small mercy. I don't need to add any more homicides to my charges.

I empty the cash register, grab more snacks, drinks and cigarettes, tossing them into the bag he'd given me for my purchases, and then get out of there.

As I make my way back to the car, I can't help but glance over my shoulder, half-expecting to see red and blue lights piercing the darkness.

My starlight is still dozing, oblivious to the chaos I left behind.

I throw the bag of supplies into the trunk, keeping a Hershey bar and energy drink, before sliding into the driver's seat. My gaze lingers on Lila for a moment. Her chest rises and falls in a slow, rhythmic pattern, the soft glow of the gas station lights casting a gentle luminescence on her features. It's a sight that brings an unexpected pang of something.

Ignoring it, I start the car and pull away from the gas station, leaving my mess behind.

Lila stirs beside me, eyes opening. "W-Where are we?" she says, rubbing her eyes.

I smirk at her. "Wouldn't you like to know?"

She sits up straighter, glaring at me. "Why didn't you take my car and leave me on the side of the road?"

Lila knows nothing about me. She's unaware that I'm a convict on the run. Unaware that I'm a murderer with no morals.

"Because I needed you, starlight."

Her eyes flash. "Why do you keep calling me that?"

"Because I'm darkness embodied, and you're my starlight."

Lila's eyes widen, disbelief painted across her soft features. "You're crazy," she breathes, leaning away from me.

The car's confined space becomes heavy with tension. I can't help but chuckle at her reaction. "Maybe I am," I counter with a nonchalant shrug. "Maybe I am."

"What's your name?" she questions, tilting her head. "You know mine."

"Ash," I reply.

"Ash," she repeats, letting the name roll off her tongue. "Why did you need my car?"

The question hangs in the air between us. I glance at her from the corner of my eye, taking in her curiosity-filled expression. "You really want to know why I needed your car, starlight?" I ask, my voice coming out colder than I intended.

"Yes," she breathes.

"Because I escaped while they were transferring me from The Metropolitan Correctional Center bound for

Menard. I'd been transferred from New York State. It was a piece of cake, to be honest. They need to sort their security out."

Her face pales. "What did you do?"

I flash her a wicked smile, my eyes glinting in the dim light. "The worst things you can imagine. Things that would make your blood run cold. You see, I don't play by society's rules. I create my own rules, and right now, you're my favorite little toy," I say.

Shock registers on her face, and she recoils. "You're disgusting."

I laugh, a deep, hollow sound that fills the car. "And yet, you're stuck with me."

I can see her struggling with her emotions, fear, and anger, battling for dominance. After several moments of silence, she finally speaks, "What do you want from me?"

I shrug, my gaze focused on the road ahead. "What do I want?" I chuckle. "Isn't it obvious, starlight? I want your fear. I want your desperation. I want you to feel the same hopelessness the world has forced upon me." I look at her, my gaze unflinching. "You're mine to do with as I want."

The colour drains from her face as she takes in my words. "You're a monster," she whispers, her voice shaky.

I don't respond. After all, Lila isn't wrong. But in this world, it's either be a monster or be devoured by one. And I made my choice long ago.

6

LILA

*T*he rain is relentless. A torrential downpour batters against the windscreen with an almost deafening force. The wipers work furiously, but they're no match for the deluge, struggling to clear the water that sheets down in thick rivulets.

Icy hailstones join the cacophony, drumming against the car's roof in a harsh symphony. The headlights barely penetrate the darkness, illuminating only a short stretch ahead. Occasionally, a vicious gust of wind sends us swerving, the tires skidding on the slick, rain-soaked asphalt. I grip the steering wheel tighter, my knuckles white. It's me, Ash, and the storm. I've never felt so alone.

Suddenly, the dim glow of the headlights falls upon an obstacle in our path. My heart skips a beat as I realize it's a roadblock. A massive tree has fallen, its thick branches barring our way forward. I hit the brakes, the car screeching to a halt just in time.

Ash stirs from sleep, roused by the sudden stop. His gaze immediately goes to the obstruction illuminated by the headlights, and he curses loudly. "Fuck!" His voice ricochets off the car's interior, almost drowning out the storm outside. The sudden burst of anger is palpable.

"We could turn back and try another route," I suggest, my voice barely audible over the storm's roar.

Ash looks at me, his expression unreadable, and then he reaches for the glove compartment, pulling out an old, weather-stained map. His fingers trace the roads, calculating the detour. His jaw clenches, a sure sign of annoyance. "The detour will add an entire day and night's drive," he declares, shoving the map back into the compartment in frustration. "We can't afford that. We'll have to detour into the woods, find high ground, and wait for someone to clear the road." His tone leaves no room for argument.

"Take the path up there," he points to an old, worn-out dust track heading into the woods to the left of the fallen tree.

I put the car in gear, my hands trembling slightly as I drive onto the narrow dirt track. The path ahead is shrouded in darkness, the car's headlights barely penetrating the dense tree canopy. Each twist and turn of the path sends a fresh wave of anxiety through me. The unsettling crunch of gravel beneath the tires and the occasional scrape of low-hanging branches against the car's body is the only sound apart from the persistent rain drumming on the roof.

After what feels like an eternity, Ash instructs me to stop. "Here," he says, pointing toward a small clearing visible through the rain-soaked windshield. It's a flat piece of land surrounded by tall trees that provide a semblance of shelter from the relentless storm.

I park the car, cutting the engine and leaving us in an unnerving silence, punctuated only by the rhythmic pattern of rain on the rooftop.

Ash is out of the car before I can speak, his silhouette swallowed by the darkness as he unloads my blankets from the trunk. He's soaked to the skin when he climbs back in, his hair plastered to his forehead and water dripping from his clothes onto the leather seats. Without a word, Ash rearranges the backseats, folding them to make space. His efficiency is terrifying as he spreads the blankets, creating a makeshift bed in the back of my Subaru Outback.

"Get in," he instructs, his voice stern.

Shivering, I awkwardly clamber into the back, my heart pounding against my ribs. He slides in beside me, his body radiating heat.

I can hear the catch in his breath as he states the unthinkable. "We need to strip down. Skin-to-skin contact is the best way to keep warm."

"No way!" The idea of this psycho pressed naked against me makes me hot for all the wrong reasons.

"This is survival, starlight," he tells me. Despite my protests, Ash's determination doesn't wane. His voice drops to an icy whisper, a dangerous undertone that paralyzes me in fear. "Don't make me get my knife and cut the dress off you." The threat hangs in the air, as chilling as the storm outside. He won't take no for an answer.

I slide out of my dress and shiver as I sit there in nothing but a bra and panties.

"Take those off, too," he demands.

I glare at him. "There's no need."

"What did I tell you?" He pulls the knife from his pocket and points it at me. "Take them off."

I remove my bra, and he groans when he sees my breasts. His eyes darken with desire as he stares at my exposed chest. "Damn, starlight," he murmurs, the roughness in his voice sending chills down my spine. "You're perfect." His gaze is fixated on my breasts, making me shudder. "Just look at those... perfect size, perfect shape," he breathes, his voice dropping an octave lower.

The words are like fingers, tracing a path down my body, igniting a fire I never knew existed. And suddenly, I don't even feel reluctant to take my panties off.

When I do, his growl is guttural. "Look at that perfect little cunt. Spread your thighs for me," he demands.

I hesitate, my body stiffening in protest. "I...I can't," I stammer.

Ash's gaze hardens, but I glare back, defiance fuelling me.

"No," I state, more firmly this time. I won't lie down and let this criminal do as he pleases. I ignore the icy fear coursing through me, the sharp coldness of the knife, and the predatory look in his eyes. I gather my dignity, pull the blanket around me, and firmly say, "I won't do as I'm told."

With a smirk, he peels off his drenched clothing. "You will once I get you hot and bothered." The wet garments are tossed casually upfront, leaving him as exposed as I am. His body is a well-hewn sculpture of muscle and ink, gleaming in the faint light.

"Lie down, starlight," he directs, his voice a gruff command that echoes in the confined space. His eyes, as dark and stormy as the tempest outside, never leave mine as I slowly recline onto the makeshift bed.

He lies down next to me and forces me onto my side, facing him. His cock, hard and pulsing, presses against my pussy. The cold of the metal piercing is evident as it rests against my heated clit. The warmth of his cock paints a stark contrast against the cold, damp air around us.

His eyes, like two nuggets of coal, watch my reaction intently, the flickering shadows playing in their depths as he awaits my response.

With a cocky grin, Ash leans in closer, his breath hot against my ear. "I bet you're soaking wet right now," he purrs.

His fingers, rough yet deliberate, trace a path down my thigh, his touch igniting a trail of heat in its wake. "Aren't you?" His voice holds a challenge, his dark eyes gleaming.

"No," I spit out, hating how wrong this situation is.

I'm so turned on, it's fucked up.

"Don't lie," he murmurs, thrusting forward so his cock slides between my thighs. And then he groans. "Soaking fucking wet. Your juice is coating my dick." He starts to slide against me, making me moan.

He grinds his stiff dick against my sensitive clit, rubbing it with the cold piercing, the friction creating a delicious pleasure. "Moan for me," he commands, his voice a heady mix of lust and assertiveness. There's a possessive gleam in his eyes, a raw hunger that has me responding before I can help it.

Each slip of his cock against my clit has me gasping. The pleasure builds, radiating in hot, pulsing waves. His hand steadies my hips, his movements firm and strategic, coaxing me to the edge of pleasure. The tight space in the back of the car fills with our heavy breaths and gasping moans, adding to the symphony of the chaos outside belting against the car.

"Ash," I breathe.

Hearing his name on my breath makes him growl. "You're my dirty little whore, aren't you, Lila?" he whispers.

His movements don't temper, the ring in his cock grinding against my clit, forcing me to fill the space with gasping moans. His dark, smoky eyes reflect a perverse satisfaction and an intoxicating dominance that both scares and excites me. "You're so fucking hot," he breathes.

His hand brushes strands of hair from my face, his

gaze intense, predatory. "If it weren't for this goddamn rain," he begins, a mischievous grin spreading across his face. "I would chase you through these woods."

The thought sends a jolt of arousal through me. "I'd hunt you down, wearing a mask, and take you on the forest floor. Even if you scream no." His eyes gleam wickedly at the idea. "I want you to scream 'no,' Lila," he growls. "I would love it if you resisted while I slammed every inch deep inside you." He pulls me closer, pressing his lips against my neck, his hips still moving as if he's fucking me.

The fantasy he's weaving is wrong on so many levels... Yet, the arousal it stirs within me is undeniable. The rhythm increases each stroke as unyielding and deliberate as the last. The friction causes sparks of pleasure to ripple through me. And then, without warning, my orgasm crashes over me so powerfully that it takes my breath away.

"You're such a naughty girl," he murmurs. "Coming undone for me while I tell you my darkest desires. They're such a turn-on, aren't they?" His voice is husky. "Perhaps you enjoy the fantasy of me taking you against your will?" A low moan of pleasure escapes him as he continues to grind against me. "Can you feel how hard you make me? How much I want to be inside you? This is all because of you. All for you."

His words are punctuated with his cock ring rubbing relentlessly against my sensitive nub. His hand sneaks up to teasingly pinch a nipple, and I gasp, arching against him.

The sinful confession and his ministrations cause another orgasm to rip through me. I've never been this turned on in my life. And I can't think right now about what that means about me and my mental state.

His laughter, raw and filled with lust, fills the confined space. "My dirty starlight wants to be raped, don't you?" he growls. "And I can't wait to explore your dirty fantasies more."

With a final, forceful thrust, he comes, his hot cum spilling onto my pussy. The intensity of the moment leaves us both spent, our breaths ragged, my body shuddering in the aftermath of two orgasms that were more powerful and consuming than anything I've ever experienced.

Suddenly, the aftershocks of pleasure give way to shame. It seeps into my consciousness like a chilling fog, causing a lump in my throat. I attempt to wriggle out of his possessive hold, but he anticipates my move.

He tightens his grip around me. "Shhh, Lila," he whispers into my ear. "You're right here, with me. My starlight." His words are laced with an unhinged tenderness I didn't know he possessed.

Despite the madness of the situation, I let him hold me. I find myself falling asleep to the rhythmic sound of his breathing, a strange lullaby that's as soothing as it is terrifying.

The car's roof takes a beating from the relentless rain outside, the sound becoming a constant echo in my dazed state. I close my eyes and let the darkness take me.

7

ASH

The morning light filters through the foggy windows of the car, casting an ethereal glow around us. As I stir from our makeshift bed, I feel my stomach rumble with hunger, the cold bite of the morning air seeping through the thin blanket. Lila remains asleep, curled up, her face a picture of innocent vulnerability.

I climb back into the front, dress in damp clothes, and start the car. It's time to move. The road should have been cleared overnight, and we must find the nearest town.

There will be an APB issued for the car by now. We must start afresh with new clothes, food, and, most importantly, a new vehicle. But it also risks people recognizing me.

An escapee, a murderer.

But it's a risk I must take.

If they catch me, then I'm going to be serving two life sentences. Basically, I'm never coming out. This means I've got to do everything I can to escape and stay under the radar. Granted, beating up a gas store attendant wasn't exactly turning over a new leaf.

My gaze drifts to Lila sleeping in the back, her peaceful slumber contrasting the storm brewing within me. I'll have to wake her once we get to a town with a general store, but for now, the sight of her calm amidst the chaos pulls at something within me. An addiction, a craving, a need that I cannot ignore.

It's strange how this innocent, sleeping woman has gotten under my skin. I could've killed her right there on the side of the road when we first crossed paths. I'd considered it, my mind quickly calculating the ease of taking her car and disappearing into the night. Yet something held me back, a glimmer in her blue eyes, a spark of something I hadn't encountered before. Something that intrigued and enticed me, making me hesitate for the first time in a long time.

I remember dismissing it as nothing more than a moment of weakness. Yet here she is, still alive, still with me. She's become my lifeline in a world that's gone mad. I don't care about her, not really. I can't afford to.

Emotions are a luxury for the free, not for fugitives like me. But something about Lila fastens me to her: a tether, a chain, a grip that I can't shake off. It's as if she's reached into the darkest recesses of my mind, and instead of recoiling in horror, she's decided to set up camp.

The road is clear, thankfully, and I drive a few more miles until the town sign for Fair Grove comes into view. I slow down a little, noticing it's a town where we can get everything we need.

I clear my throat loudly. "Wake up, starlight," I say.

She startles and sits up straight, brow furrowing when she sees we're no longer in the woods. "Where are we?"

"Fair Grove. We'll get clothes and food, and I'll find a new ride."

Her eyes widen. "What? You can't leave my car here."

I smirk. "I can and I will. Your parents will have alerted the police about your disappearance by now, meaning that the police will have an APB on your car. I need something new."

She rolls her eyes. "Surely that won't work as whoever you steal a car from will report it stolen."

I smirk as she underestimates my talent for burglary. "I know what I'm doing, starlight. I pick my targets well."

Her brow furrows. "How can you pick someone who won't notice their missing car?"

I steer Lila's car into the parking lot of a run-down-looking store. The vehicle's hum is the only sound breaking the eerie silence of the early morning. Noticing an old rust bucket of a truck parked far at the back, I smirk at Lila. "You see that truck over there? The owner probably hasn't touched it for months. That's our ride out of here." Her worried gaze makes me chuckle. "Relax, starlight. I've been doing this a lot longer than you know." I park the car and throw her dress back to her. "Put this on."

She tries and fails to keep the blanket around her as she dresses.

"Now get out," I demand.

With a deep breath, I step out into the brisk morning air. "Let's go and get supplies and make it quick." She's about to move toward the building when I snatch her wrist and yank her to face me. "No funny business, and here's the cash for the clothes you want." I place the cash in her hands and release her wrist.

Her eyes narrow. "Where did you even get the cash if you were incarcerated?"

I chuckle. "Why does it matter, starlight?"

"Because I'm not using stolen cash for my clothes." She sets her hands on her hips.

"If you don't use the cash to buy yourself some clothes, I'll just buy some for you. And you'll have no choice but to wear whatever sexy as fuck outfits I pick."

Her eyes narrow, and she stares at me briefly before sighing. "Fine."

"Good girl," I praise, enjoying how her cheeks turn pink. Flashbacks of her face twisted in pleasure while I rubbed my cock against her clit last night enter my mind, turning my dick solid. It was fucking heaven. And I know without a doubt I'll fuck her sweet little cunt soon enough. First, I must focus on getting as far away from Illinois as possible.

We make our way toward the store. It has that old-world charm with its wooden facade and rusted sign. The bell above the door jingles as we walk in, announcing our presence to the seemingly absent staff. Lila heads toward the clothing aisle, her gaze focused and determined.

I navigate through the narrow aisles stacked with everything from canned food to car parts. The scent of dust and old paper fills my nostrils as I quickly glance over the shelves, grabbing items of necessity. I occasionally glimpse Lila, her brow furrowed as she sifts through the clothes.

As I reach for a battery pack, a voice interrupts my thoughts. "Need some help there, buddy?" I turn to find a store worker, a lanky teenager with a pimpled face and a nametag that reads 'Dan.' He looks barely eighteen, his voice still breaking in that awkward phase of adolescence.

I manage a smile, hoping it screams normalcy and masks the darkness within. "Just grabbing a few essentials," I respond, my voice steady.

His gaze flicks over my shoulder, landing on Lila. I see his eyes widen, cheeks flushing. She's trying on a cardigan, twisting this way and that in front of a cracked mirror. As I look at her, my violent possessiveness rears its head. I feel a feral growl building in my chest. She's mine. Every inch of her.

"Keep your eyes off her," I command, my voice holding a dangerous edge.

He stumbles back, startled, his face turning a shade paler. "She's... I didn't... I mean...I," he stammers, his eyes wide.

I step closer to him, my gaze not leaving his. "She's mine," I growl, the words dripping with a quiet menace. "And I don't like people ogling what's mine."

Dan gulps, swallowing his words, his eyes darting around in panic. He nods quickly, muttering a low 'okay' before scampering off. A feeling of satisfaction fills me. Lila is mine and only mine. No one else should lust after her.

Lila finishes picking out her clothes and heads down the sanitary aisle. I grab a few t-shirts and jeans in the right size before following her, observing as she reaches out to touch a pack of sanitary towels. Her fingers trace the pack, her lips pursed in deep thought.

"Get some," I tell her nonchalantly, my eyes fixed on her. She startles, her hand pulling back. But she doesn't question me; she just turns back and puts a pack in the cart. I see her fingers creep toward the tampons next, and I nod in agreement. "You're going to need them at some point."

She nods, quickly adding a box of tampons to the cart. But I'm not done yet. I walk past her, reaching the end of the aisle where the condoms and lubricants are stacked. I pick up a large box of condoms and toss them into the cart. I then reach for a bottle of lube, holding it out to her.

"We're going to need these too," I say, my voice steady.

Her face drains of color, and she stumbles back as if I've struck her."Why?"

I tilt my head. "Unless you're on the birth control, and then I'll just breed that cunt of yours as much as I like."

She trembles, shaking her head.

I narrow my eyes, sensing she might be lying to me. If she were taking the pill, then she'd definitely not be covered anymore, but if she has an IUD, that's different. "Are you lying to me, starlight?"

"No," she says, glaring at me. "I'm not on birth control because my pills are at home."

I'm unsure if I believe her, but there are ways for me to check. If she thinks I don't know how to check for an IUD, she's greatly mistaken. "If you're lying to me, I'll find out." I throw more condoms into the basket and lube. And then a dildo catches my eye, so I throw it in too as it will prove useful when I decide to stretch her ass out. "Best stock up, though, in case you aren't."

Her nostrils flare. "Don't be an asshole. I don't want to have sex with you. I've got a boyfriend."

"What?" I advance toward her. My fists clench at my sides as I close the distance between us. "You've got a boyfriend?" I spit out, my voice harsher than I intended. I can feel the flames of anger licking at my insides. "Tell me his name so I can murder him for being inside you," I demand.

She flinches, and I can see the terror in her eyes. It's a sight that would have pleased me, but not after hearing that another man had been regularly fucking her before we met. She shrinks back, her eyes wide. "No!" she retorts, her defiance igniting my fury further. "I won't let you harm him."

"Is that so?" I sneer, my nostrils flaring. "Then maybe I should make you mine completely, so you'll have no choice but to forget him." My voice drops to a threatening whisper. "I can make you forget him, starlight."

I reach out, wrapping my hand around her delicate throat, my fingers applying enough pressure to let her know she's at my mercy. "I'm going to fuck you so hard, you'll forget your own name, let alone his," I promise, my words a twisted blend of anger and desire. "I'll have you begging for me, panting my name like a desperate plea. You'll find pleasure in nothing but my touch, my taste, my cock."

"Your pathetic boyfriend won't compare to the filthy, raw pleasure I can give you," I continue. My other hand slides down her side, gripping her hip tightly as I pull her against me. "He'll be nothing but a distant memory, buried under layers of lust and ecstasy. You're mine, starlight, and I'll be damned if I let him or anyone else come between us."

"You're insane," she breathes.

"You're right," I admit, releasing my grip. "I'm insane,

but it doesn't change that I want you, starlight. That I need you more than my next breath."

Her breath hitches, proving she's affected by my words. She wants what I'm detailing as much as she tries to deny it. The dirty little girl wants my dick filling her holes, taking her against her will.

"Come on, let's get the fuck out of here," I say as more people enter the store.

The cashier looks at me with an air of disinterest. He scans the items nonchalantly, avoiding my gaze. Smart man. I hand him cash.

With a silent nod, he hands me the change. I snatch up the bag of supplies and head toward Lila, standing by the exit.

"Let's go," I command. The morning air's chill counters the heat running through my veins whenever I'm near this girl.

"Get whatever you need from the car," I instruct, pulling a cigarette from my pocket and lighting it. She hesitates, her gaze flickering to the car and then back to me. After a moment, she nods, a soft sigh escaping her lips as she steps toward the vehicle.

I blow the smoke into the air, watching her as she collects the few belongings she wants to keep and returns moments later, a small carrier bag clutched in her hands.

Without a word, I approach the old beat-up truck. "This is it," I state, the rusted metal cold under my touch. With practiced ease, I break into the vehicle, the door groaning in protest as I yank it open.

The truck sputters to life a few wires later, its engine roaring in the quiet morning. "Get in," I command, my voice barely audible over the grumbling engine.

She jumps into the passenger's seat, and I pull out of the parking lot, the wheels crunching over the gravel as I drive away, leaving behind the remnants of a town that's another pit stop to freedom. We're getting closer. And I need to keep going and ensure we don't hit more hitches like the storm last night.

8

LILA

*A*sh is insane. I'm trapped with a man who's capable of unspeakable things. I don't know what he was in jail for, but clearly, he's not right in the head.

The journey is a monotonous blur of passing landscapes. The truck's tires hum a continual drone on the tarmac, lulling me into uneasy calm. Ash's face is hardened, his eyes focused on the road, hands gripping the steering wheel hard.

Hours later, the truck slows down, pulling into a barely noticeable trail leading off the main road. Following the path, we arrive at a dilapidated motel, its neon sign flickering intermittently in the encroaching twilight. It's a place that thrives on its anonymity, a hideout for those who wish to be lost in the world's crevices.

Ash turns off the engine, the sudden silence a sharp contrast to the drone we've grown accustomed to. He turns to me, a steely glint in his eyes. "We'll stay here for the night," Ash announces. He hands me a wad of crumpled bills. "Get us a room," he instructs, and I notice, not for the first time, the dwindling pile of money keeping us afloat.

Nodding, I step out of the truck, the chill of the evening air a stark contrast to the stuffy interior of the vehicle. I walk toward the motel's office, the gravel crunching under my shoes echoing in the stillness. I push open the door, greeted by the smell of stale cigarettes and cheap aftershave.

Behind the counter, an older man smirks at me, his gaze lingering inappropriately. The sense of unease I've been carrying grows as he slides a motel key across the counter, his hand brushing mine. His touch sends a shiver of revulsion down my spine. Suddenly, the door flies open, and Ash steps in, his face a mask of fury.

He lunges at the man without a word, knocking him out cold. The room is eerily silent, the only sound being the faint hum of the neon sign outside. "What the fuck was that for?"

Ash glares at me. "He was eye-fucking you." He pulls a knife from his jacket, poised to strike the unconscious man.

I gasp, stepping forward and reaching for his hand. "Ash, no!" I plead.

He shakes his head, the knife gleaming in the dim light. "He looked at you like a piece of meat. He looked at what's mine," he growls, his jaw clenching. "And, he'll call the cops. I've got no choice. It's him or me." His voice is disturbingly calm, and I realize with a sinking feeling that, to Ash, this is the only logical course of action.

I feel sick, my stomach tying itself in knots. A part of me can't believe this is happening, that I've somehow landed in this grim reality where life and death decisions are made in a rundown motel lobby.

I step forward, gently placing my hand over Ash's on the knife's hilt. "We can tie him up," I suggest. "And gag him. He won't be able to call the cops." I look into Ash's cold eyes, pleading for understanding, for mercy. "Please, Ash. There has to be another way."

Ash freezes for a moment, his gaze locked with mine. His expression softens as he studies my face. Slowly, he lowers the knife. "You really are something else," he murmurs, his voice softer. "My starlight." His words hang in the air. "The light to my dark." He pulls away from me, placing the knife back in his pocket." Alright," he says. "We'll do it your way."

A sense of relief washes over me. I've managed to save a life today, a life that was teetering on the edge.

The man on the floor grumbles. "What the fuck?" he brings his hand up to his nose and then notices us. "You better suck my cock for this, bitch," he spits, glaring at me. "Compensation for that idiot's actions."

A chill runs down my spine, the words echoing in the silence. The atmosphere turns deadly. Ash's face darkens, his eyes flaring with a terrifying rage. Like a predator pouncing on its prey, he pulls the knife again and lunges at the man, the held-back fury unleashed in a terrifying spectacle of violence.

Ash's knife carves through the air swiftly and mercilessly. The cold steel finds its target multiple times, each jab producing a ghastly, wet sound that echoes in the room. Blood begins to spray in all directions, painting a morbid picture on the walls. Life drains from the man's eyes with each plunge of the blade, his body jerking violently, then slumping lifelessly onto the floor.

The room falls eerily silent save for Ash's ragged breathing.

I stand frozen in place, a scream trapped in my throat. The room spins, a macabre carousel of crimson and terror. I want to look away, to close my eyes to the horror that unfolded, but I can't. I'm rooted in place - scared but numb.

I feel detached, as if watching this scene from outside my body. In the depth of my fear, a strange calmness washes over me, a numbness that dulls the sharp edges of reality. There's no turning back now. I witnessed a murder and the extent of the depravity that my kidnapper is capable of.

Finally, he stops stabbing him and turns to face me. His face and clothes are splattered with blood. "Sorry, starlight. Any man that even thinks about you touching his cock must die." His voice is so casual, as if he took the trash out, not murdered a man in cold blood for being a dickhead.

"You need to be put in an insane asylum."

He tilts his head. "Is that the thanks I get for saving you from being raped?"

I glare at him. "Are you fucking serious? He wasn't going to rape me, he—"

Ash cuts me off and turns the guy's computer around to show me what's on the screen. I feel physically sick as there's a video with the sound muted playing. It looks like an underage girl is tied up, screaming and crying while the same guy fucks her. "I've been around criminals long enough to know the types to watch out for, starlight. He wanted to rape you. He saw you here alone and probably got a hard dick instantly planning to rape you."

"And isn't that what you'll do to me?" I demand.

He chuckles. "No, because you want it from me, starlight. You didn't want that old man." He nods at the bloodied body on the floor. "Go to the room and take a bath. I've locked the truck, so don't get any ideas."

My brow furrows as I don't know how he can lock it without the keys.

"I'll clean up this mess." He nods at the dead body.

I nod in response and, clutching the motel key, head toward room forty-one.

Entering the room, the harsh lights sting my teary eyes. I pause for a moment, letting the cool silence wash over me. The room is nondescript, with its bland walls and plain furniture. I walk toward the bathroom with a large bathtub, which suddenly feels like an oasis in a desert.

I lock the door behind me and turn on the faucet, leaning against the bath and sliding to the floor. The numbness begins to wear off, replaced by a shiver that ripples through my being. I realize the absolute insanity of my situation, the horrifying reality I've been thrust into, and yet, I can't shake off the truth - Ash saved me.

I pull myself together, slowly peeling off my clothes and stepping into the comforting warmth of the bath. As the hot water soothes my shaking body, I can't help but ponder Ash's words. Did I really want him? Could I ever want a man who'd committed cold-blooded murder before my eyes?

My mind whirls as I submerge further into the bath, hoping the steaming water can rinse the mental turmoil that clouds my thoughts.

As I continue to cleanse myself, the warmth of the water starts to awaken a different kind of sensation; unexpected, unsettling need pools within me.

My heart hammers against my chest, my breaths becoming ragged as I reach down, my fingers brushing against the throbbing ache between my legs. My hand moves instinctively, my touch eliciting a soft moan that echoes off the cold tiles. A rush of guilty pleasure floods me.

"Ash," I gasp, my voice ringing in my ears. The realization hits me like a thunderbolt, making me freeze in the warm bath. I just moaned his name. A murderer's name.

"You called?"

I startle, about to jump out of the water when I remember I'm naked. "How the fuck did you get in here? I locked the door."

He chuckles. "I can break into a truck. Do you think a motel bathroom lock is difficult?"

I grind my teeth. "Leave me to bathe in peace."

He shakes his head. "Not going to happen."

"What do you want?" I demand.

He smirks, his eyes gleaming with a determined spark. "I need a bath, and I'm going to bathe with you."

Panic surges within me. "No, there's no room."

He laughs. "It's a huge tub; you're only little, starlight. You can sit on my lap if you'd like."

Ignoring my protests, Ash strips, discarding his blood-stained clothes on the floor. My eyes can't help but take in the sight before me. His muscled form, decorated with intricate ink, is mesmerizing. The sight of his bare skin glistening under the harsh bathroom light sends a shudder of desire through me.

An unwelcome heat spreads through my body, my pulse quickening as I take in the sight. And then he drops his pants, making me groan at the sight of his huge, hard pierced cock erect and pointing toward me. The ring threaded through the tip makes the sight more arousing and the barbell through the underside, and then I notice he's got a piercing at the base of his dick too. Another ring through it.

Regret and self-loathing wash over me as I realize how much I'm affected by him. How much my body betrays me at his mere presence. I hate myself for how my breath hitches, my stomach knots, and my core aches. I hate myself for wanting him, for needing him.

"I know what you're thinking, starlight," he says, his voice low, almost a purr. "You're thinking you'd love a ride on my cock, and I'd be happy to oblige once I find out something."

He steps toward the tub, and my protests die in my throat as he eases into the water. The steam rises around his muscular form, the heat of the water intensifying the scent of sweat, blood, and the masculine musk that's entirely Ash.

He gestures to me with a smirk, his intent clear. Swallowing hard, I hesitantly move toward him, clambering onto his lap with his guidance. His hard cock and the metal ring press against the small of my back, making me gasp.

Then his fingers find me, sliding into me with a force that makes me cry out. I can feel him deep within me, his fingers exploring me, touching me in ways that no one else ever has. His breath is hot against my ear as he murmurs, "You're a naughty little liar, aren't you? You've been keeping secrets from me, starlight." And then he gently tugs the string of the plastic device nestled deep within me. My IUD.

His laughter is low and dark. "You need to be punished for your lies," he whispers, his voice a dangerous growl that sends a shiver down my spine. "I wasted good money on condoms we don't fucking need!" There's both desire and anger in his tone.

"How shall I punish you?" Ash's voice is a menacing purr.

His fingers dance over my clit, grazing the sensitive nub in a way that sends electric shocks through my body. I groan at the sensation, my fingers gripping his muscular thighs. He starts to circle my clit, the rhythm steady and excruciatingly slow, building up an intense pleasure that makes me arch my back, gasping for air.

As I'm about to tumble over the edge into ecstasy, he pulls back, his fingers leaving a cold void where warmth and pleasure had been. I whimper, my hips bucking against him in a desperate plea for more, but he merely chuckles, repeating the torturous cycle over and over again, each time backing off when I'm on the brink of release.

The pleasure is overwhelming, and the denial even more so. His punishment is agonizingly delightful, leaving me teetering on the edge of insanity.

"What are you doing?" I growl when he does it again.

He stops. "Liars don't get to come." He moves me off his lap and then pushes me to the other side of the bath, forcing me to kneel. "They do get to suck dick, though. And I know you enjoy that." He forces my head down onto the thick length of his cock and thrusts upward, choking me. The metal ring hits the back of my throat and makes me gag violently.

Bile rises in my throat as I gag, tears springing to my eyes. I hate him, how much I love this, and how my body betrays me. He grips my hair, guiding my mouth over his length.

Pleasure spikes through me, intense and unexpected, the unique combination of fear, submission, and raw desire pushing me toward an edge I didn't know I was teetering on.

I choke on a gasp as I come undone, my body spasming uncontrollably with pleasure. It's unexpected, shocking even, but the intensity of it sends my mind spiraling into oblivion.

He grunts in annoyance, and I realize I've broken his rule. He comes down my throat, forcing me to swallow. I do; the act is a final surrender that leaves my body quivering.

"I told you not to come..." He trails off, his voice thick with desire and annoyance. He yanks me up by my hair before flipping me over onto my stomach, pushing me onto the cold rim of the bath.

A whimper escapes me as his hand comes down hard on my ass, and I can feel the sting through the haze of my pleasure. And then he spanks me lower. He's punishing me, his hand spanking my swollen pussy. After a few spanks, I come again, the pleasure so intense that it leaves me weak and trembling.

"Fuck's sake," he mutters under his breath. "How can I punish you when you come from pain and degradation alone?" He forces me to stand upright. "Get out of the bath and go to bed," he commands.

I obey without question, my body still trembling from the intense orgasms. The cold bathroom tile against my bare feet sends another shiver through me, a stark contrast to the lingering heat of my punished flesh. I wrap a scratchy motel towel around me.

He's watching me as I leave, his gaze heavy and dark with an unspoken promise. I know he's not done with me yet, but for now, I get to sleep and forget how fucked up this all is.

My cheeks burn hot with shame as I stumble toward the bed, toweling off quickly and dropping it on the floor. I slide into the bed. The sheets are as scratchy and horrible as the towel, but they're a soothing balm to my aching body, offering a temporary respite until he decides I must be punished again.

I can't help but respond to him, to the wild desire in his eyes, to the unmistakable dominance of his touch.

As I glance at the bathroom, my eyes catch the sight of his discarded clothes on the bathroom floor, the dark stains of his blood stark against the white fabric of his shirt. The sight sobers me, reminding me of the danger that lurks beneath his enticing facade.

I can't escape the reality of what he is or the danger

he poses. The man who can make me come undone with one touch is also the man who murderers as if it's the most normal thing in the world. The paradox sends a shiver down my spine, a cold dread settling in my stomach. I must get a grip of myself before I lose sight of right and wrong entirely.

9
ASH

The expanse of the country fields stretches either side of the road as we drive down the back routes toward Montana. It's taking ages, the distance between the places we've been and where we're going growing with each passing mile.

As the seemingly endless drive gets monotonous, flashing blue and red lights in the rearview mirror snap us back to reality.

"Fuck!" I say, running a hand through my hair. "Act cool."

I glance at Lila, wondering if she'd hand me over to a cop. She might. After all, I've stolen her car and forced her on this journey with me.

"Lila," I say, my voice low and threatening, "keep your mouth shut. Don't say anything unless he asks you directly, got it?"

She nods, but I can see fear flickering in her eyes.

I can't let the trooper see that. I can't let him suspect there's more to this situation than a simple couple on a trip. The paranoia that's been creeping up on me seems to explode into full-blown fear, the cop's blue uniform symbolizing everything I'm running from.

I glance at him through her side mirror, my heart pounding as I keep my hand tight around my gun, hiding it beneath my thigh.

He approaches the car with a stern expression that is at odds with the casual swagger in his stride.

"License and registration, please."

"Sure thing, officer." Lila hands over the documents, which are, of course, stolen, her hand trembling slightly.

He takes them, his gaze flicking to me. "Tail light's out." It's not a question, just a statement.

"Oh, we weren't aware, officer... I'm so sorry," Lila says, batting her eyelashes at him, trying to play the innocent damsel. It seems to work; the stern expression softens into an indulgent smile.

"Make sure you get it fixed, ma'am." He doesn't even check the license and registration. His gaze lingers on Lila for a moment too long, and a surge of irrational anger courses through me. I want to leave the car and wipe that smile off his face.

"Will do, officer. Thank you." Lila's voice floats through the tense silence, her sweet smile at odds with the fear in her eyes before.

He hands the license and registration back, tips his

hat at Lila, and walks back to his patrol car. I let out the breath I've been holding only when he's out of sight.

"If he wasn't a cop..." I start, my voice a growl, menace seeping into each word. "I'd have ripped out his throat for looking at you like that. I wanted to jump out of the car and put ten bullets in the back of his head for it."

"You're crazy if you think you can kill a cop and get away with it." She shakes her head. "You were the one that said act cool and then acted like a raging psycho glaring at him. I'm surprised he let us go."

"You're the one who's psycho," I snap back, my blood boiling. "For a moment, I thought you'd invite him for dinner!" That cop was clearly out of line the way he eye-fucked her.

"I'm not the one who kidnapped someone," she retorts, her voice shaking with a mix of anger and fear.

"Keep driving," I command, my voice steely. "And remember, you're in this just as deep now."

"I'm not in deep. If anyone caught you, the truth would be out," Lila retorts, her voice rising, her eyes fixed on the road, hands gripping the wheel. "You kidnapped me, remember?" Her voice wavers on the last word. "I'm an innocent victim in all of this."

"And yet," I say, my tone cold as ice, "you didn't seem so innocent the other night at the motel." I can't keep the sneer out of my voice. "When I had to get my hands dirty, you enjoyed it, didn't you?" I glance at her, my eyes raking over her. "You were so revved up, you couldn't keep your hands off yourself in the bath. And then you called my name."

I can almost see her squirming in her seat, but I refuse to let her off the hook. "So tell me, Lila," I continue, my voice a whisper, "who's the real psycho here?"

She shudders, and I see the flash of guilt in her eyes.

"Exactly. Case made."

Lila's eyes flash with indignation at my words, her jaw hardening as she glares at me with unspoken defiance. Yet, she swiftly redirects her attention to the winding road before us, her knuckles white on the wheel.

The tension in the air is palpable. I lean back, watching Lila navigate the endless road before us. Finally, we come to our next and possibly last pit stop.

"I want you to pull over here," I demand.

Her brow furrows because it's probably the most populated place we've stopped at so far.

"This seems a bit busy," she mutters, glancing at me as she pulls the truck to a stop and parks. "I hope you don't intend to kill anyone."

I ignore her and get out of the truck. She follows and glances around. The town is alive as they seem to be setting up for some kind of festival, but that's good. People are distracted.

"Follow me," I say. We're low on cash, but I'm desperate for a real meal. We've got about a hundred bucks left. A run-down diner caught my eye on the way in, so that's where we'll go.

I lead the way toward it, my strides steady. It's a humble place, caught somewhere between the charm of nostalgia and the weariness of time.

The faint smell of sizzling bacon and brewing coffee wafts in the air. I open the door for Lila, a small smirk playing on my lips as I watch her hesitate.

We go to a small booth at the back, crammed between the kitchen and the restrooms. The worn-out seat creaks under our weight as we slide into the booth, the grimy window providing a perfect view of the town's bustling activity. My eyes, however, are not on the view outside. They're locked on Lila.

The clatter of porcelain and the radio's murmur playing an old tune fill the air. A middle-aged woman with tired eyes and a smile that looks like it's been practiced a thousand times approaches and pours us both coffee.

"What can I get you?" she asks, pulling out a notepad, her gaze flitting between us.

"Two Bacon Cheeseburgers," I reply.

Lila clears her throat. "And a chocolate milkshake."

I grind my teeth as we can't be frivolous with the cash we've got, but after what I've put my starlight through, I'll bend the rules on this occasion.

I sip the coffee, the bitter taste lingering on my tongue. The waitress nods and makes a note of our order before disappearing back into the kitchen.

"So, starlight, how about we get to know each other better?"

She glares at me. "Are you serious right now? Why would I want to get to know you?"

I arch a brow. "Because you called out my name in a bathtub while rubbing your pretty little cunt."

Her cheeks darken, and her resolve wavers. "Don't talk like that here."

I tilt my head. "Why not? Does it get you wet?"

She crosses her arms, her eyes shooting daggers at me. "No, it doesn't. Could you stop being vulgar for one second?"

I chuckle, raising my hands in surrender. "Alright. I'll behave," I promise. Leaning back, I study her face and defiant blue eyes. "So, tell me," I start. "What are your dreams in life?"

She seems taken aback by my question, her eyes widening. But I simply wait, genuinely curious about what she wants from life. After a moment of surprise, she sighs and looks away, biting her lip. "You really want to know?"

"Absolutely," I reply earnestly.

"Well," she starts, focusing on her coffee cup, "I've always wanted to be my own boss. I love working for the newspaper, but the hours suck."

I raise a brow, intrigued. "And how do you plan to become your own boss?"

"I've got a blog," she admits. "It's been doing quite well, and I want to turn it into a full-fledged business. I write about personal experiences and have a forum where women can support each other. I've already got a couple of sponsors."

I take a moment to process this. "That's impressive," I say, truly meaning it. "So you're a writer then?"

She flushes but nods. "I guess you could say that. My mom and dad support me pursuing it as a career, but my boyfriend..."

I growl. "I wouldn't mention your boyfriend if I were you."

Her face pales, and she nods. "Fine, not everyone in my life supported me quitting my job at the newspaper even though I'm already making decent money from the blog part-time."

"Sounds like your boyfriend was a fucking asshole," I state.

"A lot of the time, he was." She looks resigned as she stares at her untouched cup of coffee. "What were you convicted of?"

I glance around, making sure no one's in earshot. "Are you sure you want to know?"

She hesitates. I see the war in her eyes as she considers the question before nodding. "Five counts of murder and three counts of armed robbery," I say, keeping my voice low.

Her throat bobs as she swallows. "And I assume you were guilty of the charges?"

I smirk. "What do you think?"

"After witnessing you murder a man, it's safe to say

you're guilty," she admits. "But, Ash, there's always a chance to change your ways."

I laugh. "Do you truly believe that? The darkness is a part of me."

"I believe anyone can change. It's never too late."

"Naive starlight." I lean back in the booth, my eyes never leaving hers. "Change?" I let out a bitter chuckle. "Why would I want to change? This is who I am. This darkness inside me, the chaos, the destruction, is all part of me." I narrow my eyes at her. "And quite frankly, I don't care what people think." The admission hangs heavy between us.

The tense silence that had settled between us is abruptly broken by the clatter of plates being set down on the table. "Two bacon cheeseburgers," she announces, oblivious to the heaviness of our conversation. "Enjoy your meal."

A wave of hunger washes over me. The aroma of the bacon is too tempting to resist. We each grab our burger and start devouring it. The tension of our prior conversation is momentarily forgotten, replaced by the satisfying crunch of crispy bacon and the tang of melted cheese.

But as I chew, my thoughts remain on edge. They ricochet around my mind like scattered puzzle pieces, disjointed and chaotic. *Why would I want to change?* I had said. But as I look across the table at her, her eyes bright and hopeful, I can't help but wonder if there is any truth to her words.

It's never too late. But is it? Would it be wrong to want something different, something more than this darkness that consumes me? The idea is foreign. The thought lingers in my mind, much like the bittersweet aftertaste of our conversation.

I am who I am. There's no changing that. This is who I've always been. Ashton Williams. The criminal. The psychopath. The kid who they couldn't control. I've raged against society all my life. No. There's no changing who I am.

10
ASH

The room is dimly lit. A single bulb swings from the ceiling, casting long, eerie shadows on the peeling wallpaper. It's shabby, but it's all I can afford for the night. I look back at Lila, her face obscured in the shadows.

She's curled up on the faded sheets, her breathing steady. I feel a strange pull toward her, a knot in the pit of my stomach. She's become a vulnerability I can't afford to have, yet I can't leave her behind.

I grab the motel phone from the nightstand, the plastic cold in my hand. I walk out the door and lock it with the key from outside to ensure Lila doesn't try to escape.

I don't wake her. I know how she'd feel about me robbing the seven eleven. Grabbing my ski mask out of my pocket, I head toward the place I'd spotted on the way in.

They'll be shut now, so breaking in and stealing everything in the cash register should be easy without any casualties. The safe might be harder to crack, but I'll try.

I pull the ski mask over my face a block from the seven-eleven. I feel my heart pounding against the cage of my ribs. Despite the adrenaline, I'm strangely calm. This is what I do best. Taking a deep breath, I blend into the shadows, the lock pick set cold in my hands.

Once at the door, I crouch down. I work quickly, the clicks of the tumblers falling into place echoing my heartbeat. The door swings open, the alarm system immediately catching my attention. No time to disable it. Speed is everything now.

The cash register isn't hard to crack. The pitiful amount of cash does little to soothe my nerves. A few hundred dollars. Not nearly enough. There's got to be a safe. But when I sneak into the back, my hopes fall flat. No safe. I open drawers on the filing cabinet and desk, searching for more. They've got to have more. Tucked away in a top drawer, however, is a locked box. It's heavy and promising. I pocket it swiftly.

Time is running out. With one last glance around the deserted convenience store, I slip back into the night, the sound of sirens echoing distantly.

Once a few blocks away, I pull the lockbox out of my pocket and use my lockpick set to open it. I smirk when it falls open. There's a gold watch, necklace, and diamond ring all of which could be sold for good money at a pawn shop. And at least a thousand dollars in cash. It'll set us up well.

I check there's no CCTV in the area and pocket the cash and jewelry, before pulling off my ski mask and grabbing a baseball cap out of my pocket. With the ski mask back in my pocket and the cap on my head, I discard the lockbox in the nearest trash can. And then I spark up a cigarette and head back toward the motel, taking dimly lit routes.

The lights of the town reflects onto the damp asphalt, the night alive with sounds. There's a bar near the motel, the neon street sign lighting up the quiet street.

Perfect.

I need a drink to calm my nerves. Throwing the cigarette to the ground, I stamp it out before entering the bar. There are a few patrons are drinking, so I keep my cap lowered over my face just in case. I settle onto a worn bar stool, the smell of cheap liquor and stale smoke familiar and comforting. I order a whiskey from one bartender and let it burn down my throat, hoping it dulls the noise in my head. I need to think.

Another bartender, a pretty blonde with a soft smile, approaches. "Can I get you anything else?" she asks, her voice syrupy sweet. She leans too close, her fingers brushing mine as she takes the empty glass.

"Just a beer," I reply curtly, my gaze fixed on the bar. I feel her gaze on me, but I don't look up, not wanting to encourage her.

"Rough day? You sure you don't need something stronger?" she teases, pulling me a beer.

"Beer's fine," I say, my tone icy. I give her a cursory glance, a clear signal that I'm not here for small talk.

She backs off a bit, her smile dimming.

In another time, in another life, maybe I'd have flirted back with her. I would've felt that spark, that excitement when a pretty woman showed interest. I would've taken her out the back, against the wall, consumed by raw, primal desire. It would've been rough, passionate, and over before it began.

And then I would've left her, another notch on my belt, another memory to drown in the bottom of a glass. But not now. No other woman, no matter how seductively beautiful, can ignite that fire within me like Lila does. Just the thought of her sends a jolt of desire through me, a longing that's become so familiar that it feels like a part of me.

She places the glass in front of me, the clink of it against the counter echoing.

I reach into my pocket, pulling out a few crumpled bills and tossing them onto the counter. The faint scent of the bartender's perfume wafts over me as I mutter a gruff "Thanks," not meeting her gaze.

There's a pause, a moment where she might have said something and tried to break through the wall I've built around myself, but then she simply turns away, leaving me with my thoughts and my drink.

The glass feels cold against my hand, condensation

beading on the surface against the worn-out wood of the bar. I take a swig. The beer is bitter, but it doesn't matter. Nothing really matters except for her. Lila. She permeates my every thought and breath, an obsession gnawing at the edges of my sanity. I run a hand through my hair.

Why not just leave her?

Why not pack up and go, leaving her alone in that dingy motel room?

But I can't. I can't because the moment I close my eyes, all I see is her. And I know, deep down, that leaving her would be the most dangerous thing I could do. Not because she'd turn me in but because I'd be lost without her.

There's a rasp of a voice behind me, breaking me from my thoughts, "Ash, is that you?" My fingers tighten around the glass, the coldness seeping into my veins at the sound of that voice.

I turn around, my eyes meeting Ian's. A familiar smirk plays on his lips. "Ian," I murmur. Though aged and worn, his face brings back memories from a past I've been trying to escape. He was a foster kid in the system with me and we used to rob places together. Until he disappeared one day with all the cash we'd robbed from a convenience store, never to be seen again.

He motions me toward the exit, his gaze never leaving mine.

I hesitate, looking back at the bar, but then I follow him outside. The parking lot is shrouded in darkness, the only light coming from the flickering streetlamp at the corner. "How are you out, Ash?" He continues when I don't say anything, "I've seen the news. There's a huge reward for turning you in."

A cold smile curls my lips, masking the turmoil within. "Well, Ian," I retort, my voice laced with a threat, "maybe they just couldn't keep me in."

His gaze hardens at my cockiness. His eyes drift to my hands, clenched by my side. "I need money, Ash," he states, a desperate edge to his voice, "I can easily make a call, you know."

I take a step closer, my jaw set. "Is that a threat?" I ask.

He swallows visibly, the flickering street lamp casting an eerie glow on his increasingly pale face. "Give me whatever cash you've got, and I'll be on my way."

My anger flares, a wildfire inside me licking at my insides, desperately trying to break free. My hands twitch at my sides, aching for a fight. Darkness seeps into my vision, a sinister veil descending over me. The psycho within enjoys the situation, a dark, deadly smile playing on my lips. "You should be careful around a man like me."

Ian's laughter echoes in the stillness. "Don't forget," he growls, "we're both criminals. We're both encoded with the same dark ink. You're no better than me." His voice carries a note of finality, an unspoken challenge hanging between us.

My eyes catch a glint in the shadows. Not two feet away from me, a metal pole lies discarded. Without missing a beat, I lunge for it. My fingers curl around the cold metal as Ian lunges at me, a snarl tearing from his throat. But I'm faster, I'm deadlier. Instantly, I'm on my feet, swinging the pole. There's a sickening thud as it connects with Ian, sending him sprawling on the cracked asphalt.

My heart pounds, adrenaline surging through my veins as I lunge forward. Before he can recover, I bring the metal pole high above my head. His eyes widen in fear, a feeble hand reaching up futilely to ward me off.

But it's too late. I bring the pole down, impaling him straight through the heart. I pull back, leaving the pole lodged in his body. A strange sense of satisfaction washes over me, the thrill of the kill resonating deep within me.

Ian's lifeless eyes stare back at me. The darkness welcomes me, wrapping me in its cold embrace, a lover welcoming me home. And like that, all my worries about Lila disappear. I know what I'm going to do. I'm going to claim her as my own. Make her mine. And I'm never letting her go. Because this is who I am.

11

LILA

*A*sh left over an hour ago.

He's taken the motel phone with him and locked me inside to ensure I don't try to escape. And, I wonder if I've lost the plot as I hadn't considered escaping.

Four days trapped with a psychopath, and I'm not even sure I want to escape. He's crazy and possessive but makes me feel like no man ever has.

Special.

As if he'd kill to keep me safe. He did kill to keep me safe. I watched him kill, and I should be horrified by it. Instead, it turned me on watching him come to my rescue.

Clearly, I need to visit a psychologist because this isn't normal.

A knock on the door jolts me out of my contemplation. The motel door creaks open, and Ash looks like a man unleashed. His clothes are splattered with blood, and his gaze is wild as he stares at me through a ski mask. His chest is heaving as if he's been running, and his hair is disheveled.

His eyes lock on mine, an unspoken question lingering there. I should be terrified, I know. A part of me is. Yet another part of me, the part that's been awakened by this man, finds it thrilling. I swallow, uncertain of what's to come.

"What did you do?" I question.

"I ran into an old acquaintance. A guy who's aware of my sentence. He was about to call the police in the parking lot of the bar, so I found a discarded metal pole and rammed it through his heart. I'd just gotten away with robbing the seven-eleven."

He says that as if it's standard, everyday conversation.

"Are you serious?"

His eyes meet mine. "Deadly. "

I realize there's something fundamentally wrong with me as I feel something stir between my thighs at the sight of him in all his primal glory, splattered in blood with a mask over his face.

What the hell is wrong with me?

"Why are you looking at me like that, starlight?"

I don't know what it is about that nickname, but it only adds to the heat coursing through my veins.

"Like what?"

He smirks. "Like you want a ride on my dick."

I clench my thighs together and shake my head. "I'm not."

"You're such a liar." He stalks toward me. "Tell the truth. You like that I kill. When we first met, I knew you were my starlight because you crave darkness. Just as stars need the dark to shine, you need me," he proclaims, stopping a foot away. "Stars can't exist without darkness. They shine brighter and fiercer when they're contrasted against the void. And you're just like them." His eyes burn into mine, and even though his words are terrifying, they have a strange truth. "You're drawn to the chaos, to the madness, to the blood. You're a star, Lila, and you need my darkness to truly shine."

I can hear my pulse pounding in my ears, the heat of his gaze, the blood on his knuckles. Even though everything in me screams to run, I hold my ground.

"I don't know what you're talking about, Ash," I say, trying to keep the tremor out of my voice. "I'm not attracted to this." I gesture to him, the blood, the madness. "I'm not into the violence. The killing."

He gives me a knowing smile that doesn't reach his eyes. "Deny it all you want. But I see the truth in your eyes." He grabs my waist and pulls me against his blood-stained clothes. "Do you like the mask too?"

I stare at him, looking into those dark eyes and wondering where my sanity went. He's right that I'm turned on. More so than I've ever been before in my life. And before the rational part of my brain can argue, I lace my fingers in his medium-length dark hair and kiss him through the mouth hole in the mask. The fabric scratches against my skin.

The kiss is ferocious, like a whirlwind of need and possession. Every caution is shredded under the onslaught of his lips on mine.

He growls into my mouth, a primal sound that sends a shiver running down my spine.

His hands roam my body, making quick work of the buttons on my blouse before roughly pulling it off. His fingers trace patterns on my back, igniting a trail of fire wherever they touch.

I moan into his mouth, surrendering completely to the pleasure he's igniting. Blocking out the small voice in my mind that tells me this is insane, wrong, fucked up.

He breaks away, leaving me gasping for breath. His eyes are dark, almost black with desire. But there's something else. A hint of menace. Yet, it's not enough to douse the fire.

"I've got something for you," he says, his voice a rough whisper. He reaches into his pocket, pulling out a length of rope. "Ever been tied up?"

I take a step back, my heart pounding in my chest. "No," I admit, realizing the idea doesn't scare me as much as it should. Instead, it deepens the ache between my thighs.

He strides forward, grabbing my wrists and tying them together with the rope. A shiver runs through me at the roughness of his touch, my breath hitching as he tightens the knot.

I look into his eyes, seeing the psycho within. And for some reason, that doesn't scare me.

"You scared, Lila?" He taunts.

"Should I be?" I throw back, refusing to let him see me falter.

His lips curl into a smirk, his eyes sparkling with twisted amusement. "Maybe," he says, leaning in so his lips graze my earlobe. His breath is hot against my skin. "But don't you like living on the edge?" His hand trails down my side, coming to rest at my waist. He pulls me closer, erasing any space that was left between us. "Get ready for a dark ride."

"Dark? How dark can it get?" I ask, the playfulness in my voice masking the undercurrent of fear.

He chuckles. "Darker than you can imagine, Lila."

"I don't doubt that's true," I respond, my voice wavering. "Can you give me an idea?"

His gaze burns into mine, the intensity of it causing my breath to hitch. Despite my apprehension, a part of me is inexplicably drawn to the danger that Ash represents. It's like I'm standing at the edge of an abyss, knowing full well the fall could destroy me, yet unable to resist the pull.

He leans closer, his lips practically touching my ear as he whispers, "Picture this, Lila: a game of Russian roulette."

His hand slips into his pocket, and he pulls out his gun, sleek and cold under the dim lights.

I stiffen at its sight, my blood chilling. "Don't worry,"

Ash says, noticing my reaction, "it's not loaded. But the threat — the idea of it being loaded — that's the thrilling part, isn't it? Especially when I slip it inside you."

Considering what he's suggesting, I can't believe the ache that ignites. Why the hell would I want a man convicted of murder to fuck me with a gun?

My face flushes crimson, and my heart races. I look at Ash, eyes wide and lips parted, unsure if I should be horrified or turned on. There's a moment of silence, and then he smiles.

"Tell me," he coaxes, gently tracing the gun barrel across my cheek, "do you still want to know how dark this can get?"

I shouldn't want this. I shouldn't desire the danger he's offering. Yet, somehow, I find myself nodding.

My mind screams at me to tell him to stop and run away, but my body wants something else entirely. Something dark, something forbidden. Desperate to prove I'm not afraid, I stare into his eyes daringly.

He rips open my night dress, the fabric discarded on the floor. He watches me, his gaze predatory, a wolf watching its prey. The silence in the room is deafening.

"You're beautiful," he murmurs, the gun still in his hand. He slowly lowers it, tracing a chilling path down my bare skin.

I shiver, biting my lip to contain a whimper. The gun is cold, its touch even colder.

"Are you afraid?"

I swallow hard, forcing a shrug. "No."

The smirk that tugs at his lips doesn't reassure me. He leans in close, the gun gliding lower. His fingers trace intricate patterns on my skin with the cold metal, each touch laced with a promise of something more.

I can't help the gasp that escapes when he lightly presses the barrel against my chest, right over my rapidly beating heart.

"There's that fear," he murmurs, his lips hovering over mine. "Isn't it exhilarating?"

I don't answer, too caught up in the overwhelming sensations flooding me. I'm aware of every inch of Ash's body against mine, every rough caress of his hand, every cold press of the gun against my skin.

"You're mine, Lila," he growls, "and I promise you, you've got no idea how far down the rabbit hole goes."

"Show me, then," I respond, surprising both of us with my daring.

"Bend over the bed," he demands.

I do as he commands, struggling with my wrists bound as I practically fall face-first onto the mattress. My body is exposed and vulnerable. I feel the cool metal of the gun tracing my skin, moving lower until it's teasing the sensitive area between my legs. I shudder at the touch, biting my lip to muffle a whimper.

"You've got the most delicious little pussy," he murmurs, his voice rough with desire, "and your clit is so damn sensitive."

The gun glides higher, tracing a path upward until it's

hovering over my ass. I catch my breath, anticipation making my heart pound.

"And this," he continues, "Your asshole is so tight, so perfect. Perfect for fucking."

I can't help but imagine the sensation of the gun inside me, the cold harshness of its touch against my most intimate area. The thought alone is enough to make me squirm in anticipation.

His fingers take over, replacing the cold metal of the gun.

With a firm grip, he begins to play with me, sliding into my wetness. "So wet for me," he taunts.

I groan into the mattress, imagining that the man behind me looks positively insane right now. He is insane, and I am, too, for wanting this. His fingers pump slowly, in and out. His thumb finds my clit, rubbing in an agonizing rhythm.

I moan, arching my back and pushing into his touch.

He chuckles, the sound as dark and dangerous as the man himself.

And then, something shifts. Ash pauses, pulling his fingers from me abruptly. I whimper, but then I hear it - the soft click of the gun's safety being released. My heart hammers as I feel the cold metal against my skin. "I think it's time we have a little fun."

Before I can respond, he moves away from me, the bed shifting under his weight. I'm left panting, my wrists still bound and body aching with need. I hear him moving around the room, a soft rustling noise, then silence. I strain to listen, trying to figure out what he's doing. Suddenly, the room is plunged into darkness as the lights flick off.

A chill of anticipation runs down my spine. I don't know what he's planning, but I'm terrified and excited.

Who knew fear could be so arousing?

The room is silent, save for the sound of my ragged breathing. Then, he's back. "Are you ready, starlight?"

Despite the fear and the insanity of it all, I realize I am ready. I yearn for this man's touch, for the madness that is him, a thirst that's as terrifying as it is exhilarating.

And then he slides the cold, hard barrel of the gun deep inside me, and I've never been more turned on in all my life. I definitely need to be admitted to an insane asylum for liking such a fucked up situation with a man who I know all too well is capable of murder. And yet, in the moment, I can't find it in me to give a shit.

ASH

I delve into the intoxicating depths of her, the metal of the gun cold but the heat of her overwhelming. I'm lost, consumed by the dark side that takes pleasure in her fear and submission to my will. I feel the tremors that course through her and the barely suppressed whimpers that escape her lips.

"There's something I need to tell you, starlight," I growl.

She tenses at my words, the anticipation palpable in the air.

"I lied." The words hang heavy between us, an unspoken confession threatening to shatter the tension. She doesn't respond, her breath hitching in her throat. "The gun," I confess, my hand tightening around the cool metal, "It's loaded. I find it more thrilling when there's true risk," I confess. The silence lengthens, filled only by the sharp intakes of her breath. I feel her muscles tense around the gun.

"The safety is on," I reassure her, my fingers ghosting over the mechanism, "But there's bullets in the barrel." My heart hammers in my chest as I await her reaction.

She's bent over the edge of the bed, her face buried in the sheets, rendering her expressions a mystery to me. But then, much to my surprise, a sound escapes her, a moan that cuts through the tension like a knife. The sound is intoxicating, sending a jolt of desire coursing through me. Her unexpected reaction shakes me to my core, pulling me further into the darkness.

It's a sound of surrender, a testament to her acceptance of the darkness that consumes us both. It's a confirmation, as if I needed it that she's completely lost in the moment. Her vulnerability and her absolute trust are the fuel to my fire.

"Do you like that, starlight?" I ask. The question hangs in the air, teetering on the edge of our collective consciousness. "Do you like living dangerously, pushed to the edge of your boundaries?" I continue, the words tumbling out as I fuck her with the barrel harder.

Her response, a barely audible moan muffled by the sheets, is all the affirmation I need.

"Fuck," I murmur, the word barely escaping my lips as my free hand moves to my jeans. I unzip them hastily, my heart pounding in my chest with a rhythm akin to a dance. My fingers wrap around my hard cock as I stroke it.

The slow, deliberate strokes send waves of pleasure coursing through me, amplifying the electricity that already buzzes beneath my skin.

I abruptly halt my movements, pulling out the barrel from her slick heat, leaving her empty and whining. Ignoring her protests, my hand travels to the nightstand, grabbing a bottle of lube I'd bought the other day from the general store. My other hand, wrapped around the dildo that I'd also purchased for this exact purpose, glistens with the slick liquid as I thoroughly coat it.

"There's a reason I bought this dildo," I tell her. The head of the dildo nudges against her tight entrance, priming her before I push it in. "Bought it just for this," I say, the words coming out as a low growl as I thrust the toy into her ass, filling her, stretching her. "How does it feel?"

She can't respond; all she can do is moan.

"How about a gun in your cunt and a dildo in your ass?" I press the gun against her tight entrance, forcing it inside. "How does it feel?"

Her moans grow louder. The sound a symphony to my ears.

"Speak, Lila," I command. I need to see her eyes, so I lift her with the dildo in her ass and the gun in her pussy, carrying her into the bathroom. "Bend over the counter so I can watch your face while I play with you."

Her eyes are dilated so much that only a tiny rim of blue remains.

"Tell me how much you like it," I demand again, my voice echoing off the bathroom walls.

Her response is a whisper, "I've never been so turned on."

"Are you turned on by fear, starlight?" I murmur, my voice distorted by the mask. The fabric clings to my face, transforming me into the faceless avatar of her darkest desires. "Does it excite you, knowing it's me behind the mask? A criminal taking what he wants?" The words hang in the air, a tantalizing question, a dare for her to admit her darkest fantasies. "Tell me, starlight," I demand. "Tell me how much you enjoy being fucked by a gun while I'm in this disguise." I watch her.

"I love it," she admits, her voice barely more than a whisper.

I growl and pull the gun from her pussy, groaning at how soaking wet it is. "You've made a mess of my gun, baby."

Her lips part as I hold it up so she can see it in the mirror.

"Do you know what I'll do with it next?"

She shakes her head.

"I'm going to fuck your ass with it. And then put my cock in that tight little cunt. Feel you wrapped around me finally." I pull the dildo from her ass. "I may have only met you four days ago, but it's felt like a lifetime. And I've wanted to fuck you since the very first moment."

Her eyes flash with fear and excitement, all her

defenses stripped away. "Ash, I...," she stammers, unable to form coherent thoughts.

"Quiet," I demand.

She falls silent as I position the gun against her stretched asshole. She tenses, her breath hitching in her throat.

I push it in, inch by inch, watching her reactions in the mirror. I see the fear in her eyes give way to pleasure, and it's the most intoxicating sight I've ever witnessed.

Once I'm sure the gun is lodged in her ass, I drop my pants to the floor.

My cock throbs in my hand as I take hold of it, smearing the precum that's gathered at the tip. With a devilish grin, I trail the head of my cock along her slick folds, teasing her entrance with my cock ring before sliding it up to press against her swollen clit.

Her toes curl, and a moan escapes her lips as I apply just the right amount of pressure. For a moment, I simply enjoy the sight of her bent over for me, face contorted with pleasure and her ass stuffed with my gun.

I continue to stroke myself against her, delighting in the way her body arches because she craves more. The anticipation in the room is palpable, and I know I won't be able to hold back much longer.

Lila, whimpering, speaks for the first time since I issued my command for silence.

Her voice is filled with desperation, shaky, and breathless. "Ash, please..." She swallows hard, and I can see the struggle in her eyes over wanting this.

"Please, what, starlight?" I ask.

"Please," she pants, her eyes glistening with need, "I need you inside me."

The words, filled with raw desire, echo in the room, setting my senses on fire. "That's my good girl," I praise her. I withdraw my cock from her folds, teasing her entrance before pushing in.

The sensation of sliding into her brings the world into sharp focus. The tight, warm embrace of her body around mine is a sensation I've craved. As I move deeper, she gasps with surprise. "Ash," she whispers, her voice trembling. It's then that she feels it – my piercing brushing against her sensitive spot.

Intoxicated by the taboo of it all, I begin to move with a rough, primal urgency. With every thrust, I can feel the cold steel of the gun brushing against my cock through her thin, delicate walls.

The thrill of danger fuels my desire, the knowledge that one wrong move and we'd both be in serious jeopardy. Every thrust and grind is a dance with death and unbearably hot.

"Fucking hell," I growl, my voice rough with unchecked lust. "You feel incredible."

"Harder, Ash, please," Lila begs.

"You want it harder?" I challenge.

Her response is a breathy moan followed by a single word that shatters any remnants of my restraint. "Yes."

I laugh. "That's it," I murmur. I can't hold back any longer. I feel my control slipping, my mind fracturing under the intense pleasure. "Beg me, starlight," I demand, my voice echoing in the room's silence. "Beg me to fuck you harder. Beg me to take you like the psycho I am."

Her eyes widen with a mix of fear and excitement. "Ash, please," she stammers out. "I want it harder." The room fills with a tangible tension. "I love it," she gasps, back arching as I fuck her. "I love it when you're fucking me with the mask on. It's like..." She hesitates, her cheeks flushing with humiliation. "I can imagine you're an intruder, raping me." Her confession hangs heavy in the air. It's wrong. It's so fucking wrong. But it's exactly what I needed to hear.

"That's it, good girl," I growl, a dark thrill coursing through me.

I push into her harder, faster, delighting in the desperate gasps and moans she rewards me with. Before long, those moans are tinged with pain as she screams my name.

"Now, come for me," I command, my voice a low growl in her ear.

I drill into her mercilessly, my fingers digging into her hips as I force her to take every inch of me beside the gun. Her body tightens around me and the gun in her ass, her breath hitching as she nears the precipice.

And then, she comes undone, her screams of pleasure echoing through the bathroom. The sight of her climaxing is my undoing. My cock explodes in her cunt, painting it with my cum, making her mine.

"Take it, Lila. Take every fucking drop," I growl, the words rolling off my tongue.

Stepping back, I take a moment to drink in the carnal sight before me. Lila bent over, the cold steel of the gun still lodged in her ass, a stark contrast to the warmth of her body. A trickle of my cum makes its slow descent from her soaked pussy. I feel a perverse sense of pride as I pull out my cell phone, capturing the scene in a photograph.

And then I look into the mirror. "Take a look, starlight. Look at what I did to you." I show her in the mirror the image of her pussy and ass. And she moans.

Fucking moans.

Perfection. It's the only way to describe this woman. "Do you like that?"

She nods, her eyes misted with desire.

"Fuck," I breathe, dancing my fingers gently down her back before grabbing the handle of my gun. Slowly, I pull it from her ass, eliciting another moan that makes my dick throb. I toss it aside into the sink and then lift my starlight in my arms.

I carry her to the bed in the dingy motel room. The sweetness in her surrender makes me want to spoil her a little. I gently place her on the bed and unfasten the rope before pulling the rough motel blanket over her.

With a soft grunt, I clamber beside her, the bed dipping under my weight. I forcefully guide her head onto my chest, her hair tickling my skin. "Rest now, starlight," I murmur, my hand gently trailing down her spine.

Within a minute, the steady rhythm of her breathing on my bare chest signals that she's fallen asleep. It's an oddly comforting sound and a sharp contrast to the chaos of my mind.

13
LILA

*E*verything feels different now. There's an unspoken heaviness in the air, shrouding us with tension. I let him do unspeakable things to me. Hell, I enjoyed them. And I'm struggling to understand that and what it means about me.

Ash is silent, his attention firmly on the road ahead. Every so often, he reaches over and gives my hand a squeeze. It's meant to be comforting, I suspect, but every touch serves as a reminder of what transpired between us. He's a murderer, a cold-blooded killer, and I allowed myself to become entangled with him.

I gaze out the car window, the passing scenery blurring into a mess of colors. I'm grappling with my actions, the guilt gnawing at my insides. The silence between us is suffocating, the tension palpable. I feel his eyes on me occasionally, his gaze heavy, but I keep my attention focused on the world rushing by outside.

"You've been quiet," Ash's voice cuts through the silence, pulling my attention away from the window. He keeps his eyes on the road, but there's an uncharacteristic edge to his voice, a shade of concern that seems alien to the man I've grown to know over five days.

"Just thinking," I murmur.

The sex was unlike anything I've experienced. Hotter than anything I've experienced, and I loathe myself for wanting to do it again.

Ash grunts, clearly unsatisfied with the lack of response. I can sense his irritation growing. It's not like me to hold my tongue. I'm usually all too eager to challenge and fight him. But right now, I feel like I'm drowning in a sea of confusion.

After a few agonizing minutes of silence, Ash speaks again. "Lila," he growls, "you need to talk to me. Tell me what's going on in that head of yours." His hand leaves the steering wheel to squeeze my thigh.

The car hums with tension, the air heavy between us as I battle with myself. I swallow hard, my eyes stubbornly fixed on the passenger side window, unwilling to meet his gaze.

Ash pulls over to the side of the road, the car jolting to an abrupt stop. He twists in his seat to face me, his eyes blazing with frustration. "Speak to me. Now."

I cross my arms, defiantly turning my head to the side. "I don't want to talk to you, Ash," I snap.

The silence is deafening, broken only by the rhythmic ticking of the truck's cooling engine.

I refuse to meet his gaze, keeping my eyes trained on the deserted road ahead. I can feel the heat of his stare. But for now, I don't care. I don't want to talk. I don't want to fight. I want to be alone with my thoughts.

Instead of speaking he grabs the back of my head and draws me toward him. His lips find mine in a searing, passionate kiss.

I try to resist, keep my resolve, and remember why I wanted to stay silent. But the taste of him, the warmth of his body against mine, the intensity of him, it overwhelms me. It floods my senses and drowns my resistance. I find myself melting into him, my anger dissipating with each heartbeat.

The kiss is intoxicating and consuming, and I lose myself in his taste, even enjoying the stale lingering tobacco on his breath. A bitter thought nags at the back of my mind. I hate myself for giving in so easily, for allowing one kiss to unravel me. But for now, those thoughts fade into the background.

A sudden knock on my window shatters the moment. We break apart instantly, our breaths ragged and hearts racing.

Ash looks up, his eyes widening at seeing the stranger outside the truck.

The hard expression on the man's face sends a jolt of fear coursing through me.

Who the hell is this guy?

Ash's hand automatically reaches for his gun tucked

into the holster he wears on his belt. "Wind down the window, Lila."

I do as I'm told. "How can I help you?"

"Get out of the truck," he demands.

Ash growls. "Why? Are you a cop?"

The stranger's lips curl up in a cold, cruel smile. "No, I'm not a cop," he replies, his icy blue gaze locked onto Ash. "I'm a bounty hunter. And you, Ash," he nods toward him, "you've been quite elusive."

Ash's face hardens, and he leans over me to address the bounty hunter. "Well, then, you've found me," he says, his voice steady and devoid of fear. The cockiness in his tone surprises me, considering the gravity of the situation. He pulls his gun from the holster, holding it loosely but pointedly in the bounty hunter's direction. "But I'm not going with you."

The bounty hunter's once confident expression falters as he sees the gun aimed at him. The power dynamic has shifted. Ash wouldn't let this bounty hunter take him away. Not without a fight.

A sudden flurry of movement, and the bounty hunter's hand shifts toward his own weapon. But Ash is quicker. The thunderous sound of a gunshot echoes in the small cab of the truck, causing my breath to hitch sharply in my throat.

Blood sprays onto my face, making me scream. The bounty hunter staggers back, a look of utter surprise plastered across his face as he clutches the red stain on his chest. His gun drops from his hand, clattering noiselessly onto the dirt road. He collapses as the life slowly drains from his eyes.

"Why did you do that?" I ask, sounding hysterical.

His jaw is hard-set as he ignores my question. "Lila," he says, his voice gruff. "Grab our things." He doesn't wait for my response before he steps out of the truck, leaving me alone with the chilling silence and the bitter metallic scent of blood.

I scramble to gather our belongings, taking one last glance at the lifeless body of the bounty hunter. I gasp as Ash effortlessly lifts the body, dragging it toward the guy's abandoned truck.

He opens the trunk and, with a final grunt of effort, deposits the man inside. The harsh slam of the trunk reverberates in the desolate surroundings.

"Ash," I call out, my voice shaking as I hold onto our bags, weighed down by the gravity of his actions.

He turns to look at me. "Get in the truck, Lila," he orders, gesturing toward the bounty hunter's vehicle.

I hesitate for a moment. But the urgency in Ash's voice leaves no room for objections. I shove our belongings into the back seats before sliding into the passenger seat.

Ash gets in the driver's seat, his hands gripping the steering wheel as he starts the truck. The engine roars to life, its grating sound a fitting soundtrack to the chaos of our lives.

I press my hands against my stomach, trying to calm the churning sensation as we speed away. I can't shake off the image of the man's lifeless body crumpled in the trunk of the truck we're now driving.

The stark reality of our situation as we flee a murder scene with a dead body sends a fresh wave of dread washing over me.

I glance at Ash, his face set in a grim mask of determination, and my mind is flooded with conflicting emotions. Fear, confusion, disbelief, and relief all vie for dominance, leaving me feeling lost and overwhelmed. I close my eyes and swallow hard, trying to block out the reality of our grim situation.

ASH

The forest looms ahead, a dense, eerie wall of trees and shadows, the perfect hiding place. The truck's headlights slice through the darkness as we go off the main road and into the undergrowth. The tires crunching over fallen leaves and twigs is the only sound in the otherwise silent woods.

Lila is quiet beside me, her face pale in the dim light from the dashboard. I can feel her fear; it's a palpable entity in the enclosed space of the truck, but there's no room for comfort right now. We have to keep moving, keep running.

As we drive deeper into the forest, I pull the truck over in a clearing, a secluded spot where the thick canopy of trees provides an eerie sort of shelter. The headlights dim, plunging us into momentary darkness soon swallowed by the moon's weak glow filtering through the branches above.

"Stay in the truck," I demand.

Lila doesn't look at me or respond as I get out and open the trunk, pulling his body out onto the forest floor. Luckily, the bounty hunter had his own shovel in the trunk, ready for me to bury him.

The act of digging is mechanical, my body on autopilot as I plunge the shovel into the earth and toss it aside. There's no remorse, only a cold, hard determination.

With the body buried and the dirt compacted, I toss the shovel back into the trunk and climb back inside. I glance at Lila, her face shrouded in shadows. I know she's afraid and not of the people pursuing me.

She's afraid of me and of what I am. A killer. But it's a part of me that I won't apologize for, not even to her.

I start the truck and drive deeper into the forest, leaving behind the grave. For better or worse, I'm the man who will do whatever it takes to win my freedom. And if that means killing, then so be it. My only hope is that Lila, my starlight, can somehow learn to accept this dark part of me. Leaving her behind isn't an option anymore.

I drive us into the heart of a deserted town, the silhouette of dilapidated buildings rising eerily in the moonlight. I stop in front of what used to be a tattoo shop, its sign barely hanging onto one rusty hinge. With a swift kick, I break in, creating a dust cloud that echoes our situation's desolation.

The store has an old generator with enough fuel to

give us light and a bit of heat. I turn it on, and the place is illuminated, making the dust clearer.

I scrounge around for blankets and create a makeshift bed in the corner. "Lie down and sleep starlight," I demand.

She lowers herself to the blankets, but instead of lying down, she sits there with her arms wrapped around herself. Slowly, she rocks back and forth.

Have I broken her?

The idea excites me in a sick and twisted way.

"I said, sleep."

"I can't," she whispers, her pretty blue eyes haunted.

"I can take your mind off things," I suggest, grabbing the ski mask from my pocket and putting it on. The words hang heavy in the air, my intentions unmistakably clear.

Power surges through my veins as I notice her stop rocking, a flicker of desire entering her eyes. She wants this, no matter how fucked up that makes her. In the dim light, she looks ethereal.

"Stand up," I demand.

She does as she's told. She's such an eager submissive, ready to bow to her king. "Good girl," I praise, taking in the image of her. "Now, strip."

I don't even have to ask her twice as she pulls her clothes off, letting them pool around her feet.

I follow her lead, pulling all my clothes off and allowing them to join hers on the floor. And then, I grab her wrist and drag her into the parlor, the chair where they used to tattoo still intact but dusty.

I clean the chair, the sound of my scrubbing echoing around the barren room. Then, with a deep breath, I lie down, my skin burning with anticipation. "I want you to tattoo your name on me."

Her brow furrows. "You're crazy." She shakes her head. "I've never tattooed in my life."

I smirk. "That makes it more fun."

I nod toward the side of the room, gesturing to the tattoo gun. "Grab that," I instruct, my voice steady.

Without argument, she moves to where I'm pointing and picks up the tattoo gun attached to the power supply. She holds it hesitantly. Turning back to me, she walks over and places it on the table beside me.

"Now check in that drawer for cartridges and ink," I instruct, nodding to it.

She walks over to the drawer and rummages through, finding some still packaged and untouched. The sterile packets glint under the light. She's found ink, too. Perfect.

"Good." My eyes never leave her. "Bring it to me, and I'll set it up for you."

I ensure the gun works first, plugging the power supply into the mains. And then I load the cartridge into the gun before filling it with enough ink.

Lila watches anxiously.

"It's working perfectly," I say, a smile tugging at the

corner of my mouth. "Now, we're ready to get started." I pass the gun to her.

"But Ash," she protests, her fingers trembling. "I can't tattoo you. This isn't a joke. It's permanent."

"Good," I reply. "Because you're a permanent part of my life. You're mine, and you're never going to escape." I pause, allowing my words to sink in and echo in the room's far reaches. My gaze remains locked with hers, conveying a deep sincerity that words alone could never achieve.

"So, have some fun with this," I suggest, a playful smirk tugging at the corners of my mouth. "Drive me insane with pleasure while you mark me as yours. Etch your name on me." The anticipation of the needle's sting, coupled with her touch, already sends a jolt of arousal through me, making my cock leak precum. I'm so fucking hard. "Make my dick leak with pleasure while you tattoo your name on me," I tell her.

Her eyes flicker with determination as she nods, gripping the machine tighter. "Alright," she concedes, her voice laced with trepidation yet palpable resolve. "But you'll need to walk me through it. I've never done this before." Her fingers trace the gun while she acquaints herself with the unfamiliar tool.

"Okay," I say, my voice steady in the quiet room. "Plug the RCA cord back in and it'll power on. Try it."

She returns the RCA cord, and the tattoo machine hums to life. She carefully positions herself, the tattoo needle poised above my chest.

"Write your name," I instruct. My heart beats wildly under the spot she's about to mark. "Don't press too hard. Just let the needle do the work. Control it, guide it, but don't push it." I emphasize the last part, knowing how easy it would be for a novice to apply too much pressure. Her eyes meet mine, a silent promise of trust exchanged between us.

As she brings the needle down, a sharp prickle of pain radiates from the point of contact. It's a potent blend of pain and pleasure that makes me groan, the sensation coursing through me, making my cock ache.

I feel the needle dance over my skin, each prick sending waves of anticipation through me. The rhythmic hum of the tattoo machine is the only sound in the room, punctuated by our shared breaths and my occasional groans. Despite the pain, my arousal doesn't wane, the intimate act of marking me as hers proving to be more erotic than I could have ever imagined.

"That's it, Lila," I manage to grind between clenched teeth, "Just like that. You're marking me as yours. I'm all yours." My voice is a low growl, barely audible over the mechanical hum of the tattoo machine. Each word, every syllable, is punctuated by a sharp intake of breath as the needle pierces the skin. "No going back now. Your name is permanently etched over my heart." My eyes lock onto hers. "Does it turn you on? Knowing that everyone who sees this will know I'm claimed. That you're the one who's marked me?"

"It does," She admits. Her eyes are locked on mine, the

soft blue depths filled with intensity. "It turns me on, Ash. Marking you in this way." She swallows hard, her grip on the tattoo gun tightening. The needle pricks my skin again, another wave of pain washing over me, followed by a surge of pleasure so potent it borders on intoxication.

"I need you to hurry up and finish so you can sit on my cock."

Her eyes widen at my words, a soft gasp escaping her lips, but she doesn't stop the rhythm of the needle. "You're insatiable."

"I want you to ride me. I want to feel you move on top of me," I growl, the words coming out in a low rumble. "I want you to take what's yours."

Her body trembles at my words. The moan she emits is pure, unadulterated desire.

Finally, she finishes. The hum of the tattoo machine dies away, leaving a silence filled with nothing but our ragged breaths. The adrenaline coursing through my veins is replaced by a searing heat as I watch her put down the gun.

"Good girl," I murmur, my voice thick with desire. "Now, come here." I stroke my cock, drawing her eyes to it. "Climb onto me. I want to feel you riding me, taking everything I can offer. I want you to take your pleasure from me. Show me how much you want this, too."

She looks me over, her gaze lingering on the tattoo that now marks me as hers. And then she climbs onto me, her soft body pressing against mine. "This is insane."

I grab a fistful of her hair, "Maybe it is," I agree, my voice hoarse with need. "But I love insane. Now ride my cock." I tighten my grip on her auburn hair enough to make her gasp and guide her down onto me. The feeling of her enveloping me is pure bliss, and I can't help but groan.

She moves above me, riding me hard and rough, making a strangled groan escape my throat. "Fuck, starlight," I hiss, my hands gripping her hips, my fingers leaving imprints on her flesh that will serve as reminders in the morning. "You feel so fucking good around my cock, baby. You're so tight, so warm."

The room is filled with the sounds of our bodies slapping together, our breaths coming in harsh pants.

A dark thought crosses my mind. It's an enticing thought that makes my cock pulse inside her. "I wish I had a knife right now," I growl, my voice dripping with desire. "A clean, sharp blade. So that I could carve my name onto your body. On your perfect, unblemished skin to mark you as mine, just as you've marked me as yours."

Her moan at my words is delicious. "I'm already yours, Ash," she breathes out, her voice ragged with pleasure.

I smirk at her surrender. "If I had a knife right now, I would make it much more than words." It's the first time she's admitted it. This girl who I kidnapped off the side of the road. She admits she belongs to me. She can leave everything behind and submit to my new world. A world where it's me and her.

Our bodies are a shaking mess, caught up in the frenzied pace we've set. The smell of sex and ink fills the room, overpowering and intoxicating. I watch her above me, the way she rides me, the way her body moves with mine. She looks beautiful and ethereal, like a pagan goddess.

"Fuck, I'm close," she whimpers, her nails digging into my chest because she's forgotten she just tattooed me there. I don't care. I love the pain. It makes me harder. She moves faster. The sensation of her muscles clenching around me sends more blood rushing to my cock.

I match her pace, thrusting into her. The world shrinks until it's just us in this abandoned room, lost in our world of pleasure.

"Come for me, Lila," I order in a gravelly voice, my eyes locked with hers. "Be a good girl, and come on my cock." The command leaves no room for argument.

A shudder rips through her body, her eyes glazed over with lust. I feel her clench around me harder, her pace becoming erratic as she teeters on the edge.

And then, as if answering my command, her body convulses in ecstasy. "Fuck, yes, Ash!" She screams my name.

Her tightness pulsating around me pulls me over the edge. I thrust into her one last time, shooting my cum deep inside her, marking her from within. I groan in satisfaction, our bodies reaching the peak and starting the slow descent back to reality.

We stay like that for a while, panting, sweaty, and so utterly sated. I pull her against me, wrapping my arms around her protectively. "I'm yours, Lila," I mutter against her ear. She shivers against me, a small, satisfied smile on her lips.

15

LILA

*A*s consciousness drags me back from the abyss of sleep, I find myself alone in the tangle of musty sheets. Blinking into the dim morning light, I turn my head to find Ash awake, standing by the derelict shop's dusty window. He's fully dressed, his back to me. His shoulders are tense. For a moment, I watch him, the surreal reality of our situation washing over me afresh.

I'm falling in love with a serial killer. Or perhaps it's Stockholm Syndrome. Who knows? All I know is I've never felt so close to someone before.

Without turning, he stiffens, indicating he's aware I'm now awake. "We need to get going," he says, his voice neutral. He finally turns to face me, his eyes holding a strange vulnerability. "We'll reach our destination today."

"And where exactly is our destination?" I ask.

He shifts uncomfortably, his gaze dropping to the

floor. "You don't have to worry about that," he says. "I'll take care of you."

"But what about my life? My family?" I ask, my voice desperate. "I can't disappear off the face of the earth, Ash. They must be worried sick."

He crosses the room in a few strides until standing before me. "Lila," he starts, his voice rough, "there's no going back," he says. His fingers dig into my shoulders, his grip iron-hard. His eyes are now shards of frozen steel. "You're mine. You're mine, and that's the end of it." His words hang heavy in the silence, a brutal testament to the reality I'm now ensnared in.

"And what exactly are you going to do with me?" I manage to ask, my voice barely above a whisper.

His eyes flicker to mine, hard and inscrutable. There's a beat of silence before he responds. "You'll be my wife," he states, his fingers gently tracing the contour of my face. His touch, despite the circumstances, is soothing. "My woman," he adds, his voice dipping lower. "My world."

His declaration leaves me breathless. I'm being asked to be the world for a man who is, by his own admission, a monster.

"But Ash," I begin, my voice trembling in the quiet room. "What if you get bored with me? What if I'm not enough for you one day?" There's a vulnerability in my question, a raw fear that he might discard me as he did his victims. "Would you kill me, too?"

The question barely leaves my lips when he jerks back

as if stung, his grip on my shoulders slackening. His face contorts with what looks like anger, but beneath the surface, I see a flicker of hurt. "Is that what you think of me?" he growls, his voice thick with emotion. "That I could ever hurt you?"

He steps back, putting distance between us, and for a moment, the room is filled with a silence so profound it's deafening. "You're my starlight, my sanity in this fucked-up world. I'd sooner die than let any harm come to you." His words hang in the air, an unspoken promise in the depth of our shared darkness. "Let alone hurt you myself."

"I can't help but think it," I assert, holding his gaze. "I've seen how easily you can kill." My voice cracks at the last word as flashbacks of the blood and gore I've witnessed hit me hard. Blood and gore that this man is responsible for.

How can I be alright with that? How can I be okay with that part of him?

He ponders over my words, his gaze distant and unreadable.

Finally, he breaks the silence. "I understand your fear, your hesitation." He steps toward me but stops short. "I wish I could change who I am, what I've done. But I can't." His eyes hold a tempest of regret and something akin to longing. "You're my tether to sanity, Lila. Killing you would be like killing myself."

He runs a hand through his hair. "I can't promise you I won't kill again. But I *can promise* you this: I'll never hurt you. And if you want to leave," His chest heaves as if saying it hurts him. "I won't stand in your way, not anymore."

I'm left grappling with the terrifying reality of my feelings for this man—a monster who, despite his brutal nature, holds my heart in his hands. "I don't agree with the killing." My words hang in the air, unfinished, as I grapple with the complicated web of emotions within me. There's fear, disgust, and a distinct warmth, an affection that I can't quite quell. A part of me wants to flee, to separate myself from this cold-blooded killer. Yet, another part that feels alarmingly at home in his company urges me to stay. "But I can't ignore what I feel for you," I confess. "I can't... I won't leave you."

His expression, previously hard and unreadable, softens. The tension in the room dissipates, replaced by a quiet understanding. Love thrives even in the darkest corners.

He moves closer, closing the distance between us. His arms wrap around me, strong and protective. The world around us falls away, leaving nothing but the two of us and the connection that binds us. Then, he leans down, his lips meeting mine in a kiss that's as gentle as it is fierce. It's a kiss born of desperation and longing, a silent affirmation of our twisted love.

When he breaks away, his eyes are full of more emotion than I've seen since we met. "No promises of a fairy-tale ending, starlight," he admits, planting a soft kiss on my forehead, "but I can promise you I'll strive to be a man worthy of you."

I look at him, my heart pounding as I search his face for any sign of deception. But all I see is sincerity, raw and unmasked. A hope ignites within me, one that I'd been too afraid to kindle before. We can find our version of happiness, however unconventional it might be.

A sudden pang of guilt washes over me, a stark reminder of the other lives intertwined with mine. My parents. They must be worried sick, their imaginations conjuring up the worst possible scenarios. They deserve to know I'm safe, at the very least.

"I need to let my parents know I'm okay," I whisper.

He nods, an understanding in his eyes. "We'll find a way to get the message to them without drawing suspicion."

My throat bobs. "Can't I use a payphone here?"

Ash's jaw clenches. "It would alert the police to your location, and they'll be looking for you."

"But we'll be gone before the Chicago police can even get people onto us," I say, hoping he'll at least give me this.

He nods. "Fine." He clears his throat. "We need to get our things and get out of here, but we're going to have to ditch the truck."

"Ditch?" I confirm.

Ash nods. "Yeah, I saw an old abandoned truck on the way in. We'll steal it, load our things in, and then I'll drive the other into a lake. We can't have it tying us to the disappearance of the bounty hunter."

We quickly set to work, gathering our belongings and loading them into the abandoned truck, which wasn't even locked. The abandoned shops turn out to be a treasure trove of supplies. Ash gathers enough gas in jerry cans to last us a while.

Once we're ready, he points toward the payphone at the corner of the street. I walk over to it and get inside. My hands tremble as I reach for the receiver. I insert the coins, the metallic clink echoing the pounding of my heart. The dial tone lasts an eternity, and when the second one ends, my mother's frantic voice echoes through the line. "Hello?" she says.

"Mom, it's me, Lila," I say, trying to keep my voice steady. There's a long pause and an audible gasp at the other end of the line.

"Lila? Is that really you? We were so worried..." her voice trails off, filling with relief.

"Yeah, Mom, it's me. I'm okay," I say quickly. "I'm really sorry I missed the party. I lost my phone and..." The lie tumbles out easier than I thought it would. I take a deep breath before continuing.

"I had this argument with Brian, and I needed some time to clear my head," I add, injecting as much normalcy into my tone as possible. I can almost see her nodding, processing my words, and I let out a breath I didn't know I was holding.

"Where are you?" she asks.

I clear my throat. "I took a drive down south, and I'm taking a vacation. I need some space from Chicago and Brian right now."

"Okay, I told the police you were missing. I'd better tell them you're fine."

"Yeah, I really am. I'll get a new phone and let you know the number once I do."

"Okay, sweetheart. Just take care of yourself," she says, her voice quivering. "We miss you, and we love you."

"I love you too, Mom," I say, a lump forming in my throat before hanging up.

I hang up the phone. My throat tightens as I contemplate the enormity of what I've done, of the decision I've made. I've chosen to exist in this strange new world alongside Ash, a man whose past is stained with violence and blood.

I swallow hard, realizing that I may never see them again, never hear their voices in person. The weight of my choice sits heavy in my chest. The world I once knew feels like a distant dream fading fast.

I wipe away an errant tear, bracing myself for the journey ahead, for a life with a convicted murderer. The payphone feels cold in my hands, echoing my chosen future.

Am I making the wrong decision?

16

ASH

*O*ur convoy of two snakes its way through the empty country roads. The engine's hum is the only sound accompanying me, a rhythmic lullaby amidst the enveloping silence.

I can see Lila's silhouette in the rear-view mirror, her face illuminated in the glow of the dashboard lights. I swallow hard, my fingers tightening on the steering wheel. Being with her, and caring for her, it's like walking on a tightrope. One wrong move and I risk falling into a chasm of emotions I've spent my life avoiding. I try to push these thoughts to the back of my mind, focusing on the road ahead and the truck I need to dispose of.

Caring about someone is a concept so alien to me. I've been on my own for as long as I can remember. My dad died when I was just a baby, and my mom chose the seductive allure of heroin over raising a four-year-old.

Dumped at a foster home, I learned early to rely only on myself, to build walls around my heart. Now, every glance at Lila chips away at those walls, stirring something in me I don't quite understand, a thrilling and terrifying sensation.

The lake emerges in the distance, its surface glistening under the vestiges of the day's light. It's eerily serene, starkly contrasting the turmoil within me.

I park close to the water's edge, the crunch of gravel under the tires breaking the silence. Lila parks a little distance away.

Stepping out of the truck, the cool night air hits me. The crunch of gravel under my boots seems loud in the quiet stillness. I scan the area for a rock, large and heavy enough for my purpose.

From my peripheral vision, I see Lila step out of the other truck, her silhouette illuminated faintly by the moonlight. Without uttering a word, she joins me, her boots crunching on the gravel in rhythm with mine.

Finally, my fingers brush against the rough texture of a rock lodged in the ground. I pull at it, muscles straining, and it finally gives way.

"Get back in the truck, starlight," I order.

Lila hesitates, her brow furrowing. "Ash, I can—" she starts.

But I cut her off. "Just get in the truck," I repeat.

With a final glance in my direction, she nods and climbs back into the truck. I watch as she pulls the door shut.

Turning back to the task, I enter the bounty hunter's vehicle. I turn over the engine, the rough purr of the motor coming to life.

I look down at the rock in my hand, its rough texture grounding me in this surreal moment. Carefully, I place it on the accelerator pedal, adjusting its position until I'm satisfied it will do the job.

Taking a deep breath, I open the door and exit the vehicle. In a swift, practiced motion, I reach into the cab and shift the truck into drive. It jolts forward, crunching gravel beneath its tires fills the air. I jump out of the way, watching as the truck lumbers toward the lake, its headlights cutting through the night like twin beacons.

The truck picks up speed, its bulky frame swaying as it barrels toward the lake's edge. Then, it plunges into the lake with a startling crash and a water spray.

I watch as the truck slowly sinks beneath the surface, the last of its lights winking out as it gets swallowed by the cold, dark depths.

The ripples on the water grow calmer, and soon, there's nothing left to indicate the vehicle was ever there. All that remains is the still lake, its surface gleaming under the dusky sky.

I glance back at Lila, who watches the spectacle from the truck. Her expression is impossible to decipher. Turning my back on yet another mistake to add to a long, violent list, I walk back to her and get into the driver's seat, placing a hand on her thigh and squeezing.

"We'll drive a couple more hours and then sleep in the

truck," I announce. "Then we'll only have a few more hours tomorrow morning until we reach our destination."

"Are you going to tell me where exactly our destination is?"

"I own a cabin in the woods. Although it's not registered in my name. It was my dad's, and it remained in his name when he died. Some screw up with paperwork, meaning they shouldn't trace it back to me."

"Why are we going there?"

"Because it's safe," I respond, keeping my eyes fixated on the road ahead. My grip tightens on the steering wheel as I say, "And because we can start a life there together."

After that, she doesn't say anything, her gaze shifting toward the passing scenery. We drive in silence, each lost in our own thoughts.

With Lila by my side, it feels as though I've been given a second chance. A chance to right the wrongs of my past or at least stop the violence and chaos I reap wherever I go.

ASH

*A*s the sun rises, we venture further into the rustic trails that lead to the cabin. The wilderness is thick here. The air is rich with the scent of damp earth and pine. It's a terrain with few intruders, its serenity only interrupted by the occasional rustle of wildlife.

The dense foliage muffles the truck's engine. As we delve deeper into the woods, the boundary between civilization and wilderness blurs until it's just us, the truck, and nature. The cabin is hidden in this labyrinth, a secret haven known only to me.

For a moment, I consider the implications of bringing Lila here to this isolated remnant of my past. But the reality of our situation leaves me no choice. As the truck cuts through the morning mist, the sight of the cabin emerges, a plume of smoke spiraling from the chimney into the cloudless sky.

"What the hell?" I growl, noticing the logs stacked at the front of the cabin. "Someone's in my cabin."

Lila sucks in a shaky breath. "That's not good. Do you think it's an intruder?"

I nod. "It's been abandoned for so long someone must have decided to fix it up and squat." I crack my neck. "We'll have a fight on our hands."

Lila pales. "More murder?"

"I can't let someone who broke into my home get away with it." A surge of adrenaline courses through my body, sharpening my senses.

I've faced monsters before, but this feels different. This cabin has always been a sanctuary. To have that violated is a different beast altogether.

I park the truck a safe distance away, my gaze locked on the plume of smoke. "Stay here," I tell Lila.

She opens her mouth to protest, but before she can, I kiss her.

"Don't argue."

She sighs heavily. "Fine." She crosses her arms over her chest.

I can't help but think I'd love to beat that bratty attitude out of her. Pull her over my knee and spank her ass until it's red. "Good girl," I murmur before getting out of the truck and pulling my gun from its holster.

With cautious steps, I approach the cabin, the crisp crunch of leaves beneath my boots echoing ominously. The scent of burning wood fills my nostrils, a stark reminder of the foreign presence in my sanctuary. As I reach the cabin door, my grip tightens around my gun.

Without hesitation, I kick in the door, splintering the aged wood. "Who the fuck are you?" I demand, aiming my gun at the unkempt figure who looks at me with alarm from where he's seated by the fire, a worn-out blanket draped over his shoulder.

The intruder is a man, grizzled with age and he meets my glare with a steady gaze.

"I'm the owner of this cabin," he states.

"Bullshit," I retort, "the old man's been dead for thirty-two years."

The man sighs, a soft chuckle escaping his lips as if amused by my ignorance. "Your mom always had a flair for the dramatic," he mutters.

My heart thuds against my rib cage. "What the hell are you talking about?" I demand, my grip on the gun tightening.

He meets my gaze. "Son," he states, his voice barely above a whisper, "I'm Liam, your dad."

A bitter laugh escapes my lips because of the absurdity of his claim. "Impossible," I spit out, my anger flaring. "You're lying!"

He shakes his head. "It's not a lie. My name's Liam Williams, husband to Donna Williams and father to Ashton Williams."

Rage, confusion, pain. I shake my head, unable to accept his declaration. "No," I growl, clenching my teeth, "he's dead."

And with that, the room falls silent, the crackling fire the only sound punctuating the tense quiet. The emotions churning within me are complex, complicated by years of abandonment and the bitterness of betrayal.

"I know your mother died from a heroin overdose when you were five," he begins, his voice heavy with regret. That's news to me. All I know is that she dumped me at a foster home when I was four. "I'm sorry I left you with her, but I wasn't cut out to be a father either." The admission tastes like bile in my mouth, the harsh reality of his abandonment hitting me like a freight train. "I had my demons," he adds.

He meets my eyes once again, his expression grave. "And I know you've fallen victim to your upbringing, considering there's a nationwide manhunt for you." His words hang heavy in the room's silence, a stark reminder of my failings. There's a quiet moment before he continues, "When I saw the news, I knew you'd be heading here."

"And what do you want from me now?" I snap.

His gaze is fixed on me as if weighing his words carefully. But I'm not looking for calculated responses or well-crafted lies. I want the truth. "Just spit it out!"

"I want a chance to make things right," he murmurs.

I stiffen, my heart pounding in my chest. The audacity of his request is staggering. The blatant disregard for the past, for the life I've had to endure because of him, is maddening. I feel the anger bubbling up inside me, hot and raw. "You think you can waltz back into my life and fix everything?" I spit out, my voice icy. "You don't get to show up and play the hero, Dad." The word 'dad' sounds foreign on my tongue.

"I know I can't fix things," he admits, his voice steady. "But I can offer you a safe place, a haven." His gaze moves toward the window. "I've got a home in Alaska, much larger and safer than this. You can have it." My eyebrows furrow in surprise, but I stay quiet, listening. He continues, "I've been running too, Ash. From crimes, from my past. I've built a cabin up there on the same land." His voice is barely more than a whisper. "I'll live there. We don't have to see each other unless we want to. You can have your peace, and I can have mine." His words hang in the air, a proposal that's as unexpected as it is tempting. I know staying here in Montana is dangerous. The authorities could catch up to me, but Alaska is a different beast entirely.

"I'm with someone. She'll have to come to," I demand.

He nods. "Of course."

"And if you even think of trying to rat me out, I won't hesitate to murder you."

His eyes flash with sadness. "You think I'd rat out my only son?"

I shrug. "I don't know you. You abandoned me, didn't you?"

He accepts the barb, his eyes downcast. "Yes, I did. And that's something I'll always regret." His words are heavy with remorse, but it doesn't erase the past.

It doesn't erase the pain, the abandonment. Trust isn't

something that can be won over with a few regretful words. It's earned, and he's got a long road ahead of him if he thinks there's even a sliver of a chance that I'll trust him. I have my demons, but these are the ones that haunt me.

LILA

*a*sh and I sit quietly in the warmth of the cabin's living room, the only sound being the faint crackling of the fire dancing in the hearth. The flickering light casts long shadows across Ash's face. His gaze is focused on the dancing flames, but I can tell he's far away, lost in the labyrinth of his thoughts.

The atmosphere is thick with tension and a silent battle of emotions. I reach out, brushing my fingers against his, a simple act of solidarity.

"I..." Ash stammers, pulling his hand away from mine and leaving a cold void. His eyes, stormy and conflicted, meet mine, searching for something I'm not sure I can give. "I can't do this. Not now."

I reach out again, this time, he doesn't withdraw, but the tension in his body tells me he's on the edge.

"I understand, Ash," I speak softly. "This is hard for

you." I pause, looking at him intently. "But I can take your mind off things."

He stiffens, hearing me using the same phrase on him as he used on me. "Can you?"

I nod and climb into his lap, grinding myself against his already stiffening erection. And then I kiss him.

He grabs the back of my neck forcefully. "Careful, starlight. I'm not in a good mood, which means I'll ruin you."

I moan at his forcefulness. "If that's what you need, then ruin me."

"Fuck," he mutters against my lips. "I don't fucking deserve you, but I'll take you anyway."

And then he kisses me more deeply, more ferociously than ever before. His tongue searches my mouth as if his life depends on it. I let him take what he needs from me. I no longer question why I'm so drawn to a man as unhinged and psychotic as him. A part of me fears it's because of my past.

What if my childhood trauma is the reason why I'm so drawn to Ash?

I don't even want to go there. Some things are best left buried.

Ash breaks the kiss, panting heavily. "Let's play a game. You run. I chase." His eyes hold a dangerous glint that sends a shiver down my spine. "Are you up for that?"

I lean back, studying his face, wondering if I'm crossing a line I shouldn't ever cross, particularly with a man as dark and psychotic as Ash. But I know he needs this. Maybe I do, too. So, I nod, swallowing hard. "Alright."

He smirks, a dark, predatory look that sends a thrill coursing through my veins. "But what are the limits, Lila? How dark can I be with you?" He leans into my ear. "How about consensual non-consent?"

"What?" I pull back, confusion flickering in my gaze. "What do you mean?"

"Consensual non-consent. It's a role-play. I pretend to be a stranger. You play the damsel. Even when you say 'no,' I continue. But it's all a game. You can stop it at any time with a safe word. What do you say?"

A shudder runs through me, a strange mix of fear and anticipation. A part of me is screaming to run, to get away from this dangerous game and man. But another part, a darker, more primal part, is drawn to it. Drawn to him and his darkness, the raw intensity that radiates off him.

"Yes," I whisper. "Let's do it." I take a deep breath and pull away from him. "There are no limits. Do whatever you want."

His eyes flash at that. "Are you sure, starlight?"

I take a moment, looking deep into his eyes. "Not exactly," I admit, my voice trembling. "But I want this, I think. I want to explore this with you." I see a flicker of something in his eyes. Surprise? Relief? It's hard to tell.

"Safeword is Cherry," he breathes into my ear. "Now run for me."

I scramble off his lap and bolt toward the door, running out of the cabin into the thick forest. Behind me, I can hear Ash counting down from ten, the thrill of the chase igniting something raw and primal within us both. And then, the chase begins.

The night is pitch black, the forest alive with a thousand different sounds. I stumble through the underbrush, twigs snapping beneath my feet. The fear and exhilaration send my heart pounding in my chest. My breath comes in ragged gasps as I try to quieten my footsteps, but the rustling leaves underfoot give me away.

Ash's voice echoes through the trees, "Darkness is coming for you, starlight!" His footsteps sound too close considering he only just started chasing.

A sudden rustle nearby jolts me out of my thoughts. I sprint toward a denser section of the forest, my heart pounding as if trying to escape from my chest. I can barely see where I'm going, but I push onward, the adrenaline fueling my panic-stricken flight.

"Starlight, where are you..." His voice is closer.

And then I feel it. A firm grip on my wrist sends a jolt of electricity coursing through me. I whirl around, coming face to face with Ash in a different, skeletal mask. His eyes are dark, filled with a predatory hunger that sends a shiver down my spine.

"Got you!" He breathes, his voice husky with desire and exertion. His grip on my wrist tightens, pulling me closer. His breath fans my face, hot and quick, matching the rapid throb of my pulse. "You can run, starlight," he murmurs, "but you can't hide from me."

He pushes me up against a tree, the rough bark digging into my back.

I gasp as he pins my hands above my head. "Let me go!" I command, my voice trembling. "You psycho! Let me go."

He stares at me through the eye holes of the mask. The eerie appearance is further enhanced by the dark forest backdrop. He moves closer, his lips brushing the shell of my ear. "I'm going to take you while you scream no. I'll fill you with my cock and make you come so hard you won't be able to form the word no anymore."

I shudder, shaking my head. "No, I don't want this. Leave me alone."

"I'll conquer every inch of you, claim you in ways you've never been claimed before. I'll make you mine in a symphony of pleasure and pain. You'll know nothing else but me when I'm done with you."

His hand slides down my side, his touch igniting a fire within me despite the night's chill. I struggle against him, our little game feeding into the tension that's been building between us.

Despite my resistance, I can feel the pull, the all-consuming desire that makes my heart pound even harder in my chest.

His lips descend on mine, a savage and brutal invasion that leaves me breathless. The metallic taste of blood fills my mouth as his teeth graze my lip. The mix of pain and pleasure sends a thrill through me, a dark and twisted sensation that adds fuel to the fire raging within me. "Please...no..." My protests are weak, tears stinging my eyes as I fight him.

In a swift, deft motion, he tears away the last barrier between us, my panties giving way to his rough touch. He unbuckles his belt, freeing his cock

He presses against me, the hard length of him hot against my thigh.

I whimper, my body trembling against his. His lips find my neck, biting and suckling the sensitive flesh there. The sharp sting of his teeth forces a gasp from my lips.

I twist in his arms, trying to escape, but his grip is unyielding. "No, please stop..." My plea is a whisper, an echo in the night.

But the look in his eyes tells me he's far from finished.

"I can't stop," he growls against my neck, a low, dangerous rumble that sends icy shivers down my spine. His hand tightens around my waist, his grip almost painful. "I'm a monster. A beast with an insatiable hunger. And you're my prey."

I know a sane person would be terrified, and part of me is, but there's another part of me, a dark and dangerous part, that yearns for the savage intensity of this monster.

With a swift, brutal movement, he slams into me. An unexpected shock courses through me, and I scream,

"No, stop!" My voice echoes through the forest, a desperate plea carried away on the wind.

But he doesn't stop. Instead, he moves deeper, and the metal of his piercing hits the perfect spot inside me. I never imagined how good it would feel to be fucked by a guy with a cock piercing. And each thrust rubs the ring at the base of his cock against my clit.

The rough bark of the tree scrapes against my back as he thrusts harder. I bite my lip, suppressing a moan. I clench my hands into fists, nails digging into my palms, trying to maintain the illusion of resistance.

The sensation of him filling me is overwhelming and intoxicating. It's nearly impossible not to let the pleasure take over, not to succumb to the desire that's coursing through my veins. But I force myself to continue the pretense and keep up the façade of not wanting this, even though I've never been more aroused in my life.

"You like this, don't you?" he growls, his voice throaty and rough. "You like me taking you like this, in the middle of nowhere, where no one can hear you scream." His words send a thrill down my spine, intensifying the pleasure coursing through me.

"No," I spit out.

His pace is unrelenting, each movement a searing reminder of his control.

"You're a liar," Ash breathes out. "I can feel your cunt squeezing me. It's soaking fucking wet. You love me raping you, and I want to do this every day for the rest of our fucking lives."

He bites my lip hard. The sharp pain intensifies the pleasure.

The taste of copper fills my mouth, the bite drawing blood. His savagery thrills me. I can't help but react, my body complying with his, mirroring his intensity. Yet, I keep fighting, retaliating with an equally savage bite to his shoulder. His groan vibrates against me, the sound as erotic as the act itself.

"Is that all you've got?" he taunts. And then he drops me onto the floor, the cold, damp earth beneath me a stark contrast to the warmth of his body. His body over mine as he pins me to the ground with his weight. "I bet you're aching for me, aren't you?" Ash says, his voice laced with raw desire. "You want me to fill you up, invade you, claim you as mine."

Before I can respond, he thrusts his cock inside me, a violent assertion of his control.

His grip on my wrists tightens, pinning me down as he increases the pace of his thrusts. Each one is harder, deeper, an unyielding assault pushing me closer to the edge. "You want to fight, Lila?" he growls, the threat in his voice only adding to the raw, animalistic desire coursing through my veins. "Then fight."

I do fight. I buck beneath him, my nails clawing at the earth as I try to find some leverage. But my struggle only fuels his desire. He grunts, the sound echoing through the night as he fucks me with a savagery that matches my resistance. My body rocks with the force of his movements, my cries of pleasure and protest swallowed by the darkness.

His rhythm is punishing, each thrust intended to deepen his claim over me. "You're mine," he rasps out.

I can feel him everywhere. His presence all-encompassing. The push and pull, the pain and pleasure, they all combine into an exquisite torment. And I love it. But I won't stop fighting.

"Stop," I gasp out, even as the wave of my orgasm crashes over me.

He laughs, the sound dark and uncontrolled against the forest's quiet. "You're fucking crazy," he tells me. "You scream at me to stop while your cunt squeezes my dick, milking me for all I'm worth." His hands grip my hips tighter, his thrusts slowing but not stopping. "I love your crazy," he grunts.

His words hit me like an unexpected wave, sweeping away the last of my defenses. I don't know what the fuck I feel for this man. Is it Stockholm Syndrome? Possibly. I've never felt so intensely connected to another person in my twenty-seven years. In his arms, I feel free and uninhibited.

His eyes meet mine with a dark promise. "I'm going to fill you with my cum," he declares, his words punctuated by a particularly powerful thrust that has me crying out. "Pump your tight little pussy full of it."

Then, with a primal growl vibrating against my neck, he bites down. The sharp, sudden pain is amplified by the intense pleasure radiating from my core.

I gasp, my body arching involuntarily as his cock twitches inside me. And then I feel the warm flood of his cum. His arm wraps around my waist, keeping me pressed against him as he continues to pump into me, marking me as his. The pulsating warmth spreads, and I can't help but squeeze around him, reveling in the feeling of being so intimately claimed.

As the pleasure and adrenaline recede, I'm hit by overwhelming emotions. I start to sob, and Ash stiffens, quickly pulling out of me and scooping me up in his arms.

"What's wrong, starlight? Did I hurt you?"

"No," I choke out between sobs, shaking my head vigorously. "You didn't hurt me."

His worried expression doesn't fade while he carries me back to the cabin. He settles into an old rocking chair on the porch, cradling me in his arms as we rock back and forth in a comforting rhythm. His touch is gentle and soothing, but the tears don't stop.

"Why can't you stop crying? What's wrong?" he demands.

I take a deep breath, trying to slow the wave of tears, knowing I need to explain. "It's because of my past, Ash," I start, choking on the words. It feels like I'm standing on the edge of a precipice, and it's terrifying. But I can't keep this hidden any longer, not from him. "My uncle abused me when I was a kid. Until my parents caught him trying to... trying to..." I trail off, knowing it doesn't need to be said.

Ash's grip on me tightens, his body rigid as if physically struck by my words. "How old were you?"

I cast my eyes, ashamed even though I know it's not my fault. "Seven when it started. I was Ten when my parents caught him."

His jaw clenches, and rage ignites in his eyes. "That fucking piece of shit!"

I clutch onto him. "It's so long ago, but I'm scared I'm drawn to you because..." I trail off, unable to say the words.

Because I'm damaged by my past.

"I'm going to kill him for harming you," he says, holding me tighter. His hands ball into fists, his knuckles turning white with the intensity of his grip. "I'm going to enjoy the warmth of his blood on my hands and watching as the light leaves his eyes." His rage is not directed at me but at the man who stole my innocence. I clutch onto him tighter, letting his strength and determination engulf me like a protective shield.

I shake my head, tears blurring my vision as I bury my face into his shirt. "You can't," I mumble through a sob, my words muffled. "He's already dead. He died five years ago in prison."

The tension in Ash's body slowly ebbs away. He takes a deep breath, exhaling slowly as he processes the truth. "Dead," he repeats, the word like a bittersweet poison on his tongue. "I can't bring him back to make him pay, Lila," he says, his voice thick with restrained fury. "But I promise you, I'll do everything I can to help you move past this." His voice is firm, his resolve unwavering. "Because you're my world. My reason for fucking living. I would kill any man that ever tries to touch you, understand?"

I nod, holding him tighter. This man might be a convict, a murderer, and psychotic, but for the first time in a long time, I feel genuinely understood and genuinely cared for. It's not a sufficient balm for the wounds of the past, but it's a start and a step toward healing.

1 9
ASH

$\mathcal{I}$ wake to the murmur of low voices coming from the living room of the cabin and an empty bed. My gut churns with protectiveness. I push the sheet aside and stand, getting dressed. Then I head out of the bedroom.

Lila is chatting to my dad. I don't like seeing anyone close to her, even if it's my father, my presence immediately halting their conversation. "Morning," I grumble, looking from Lila to my dad.

"Your dad was explaining how beautiful it is where he's built his home," Lila says, her eyes flicking between us.

"Yeah, but you guys better have something to eat." He nods at a pan of cooked bacon and pancakes plated on the side." My dad clears his throat, drawing my attention to him. "As we've got a very long journey ahead of us."

He isn't kidding. Alaska is at least a thirty-five-hour

drive, and I don't believe his place is just over the border. "Yeah, how's that going to work exactly?"

His jaw clenches. "We'll take my truck and yours. They both should have good fuel tanks that'll get us from gas station to gas station when we get more rural. We'll keep a few cans of gas in the back."

Good. I'm glad we won't be riding in the same vehicle as him.

"We'll have to take quite a few pit stops. I assume you've done the journey before and know the best places?" I confirm.

Dad nods. "Yeah, I've got a map with all the stops. It will be a tough five or six days in total."

"Just know, I'm not forgiving you for abandoning me. I'm accepting because it's safer for me and Lila." I glare at him, the anger over my abandonment consuming me as I stare into his eyes. Eyes that look exactly the fucking same as mine. I can't believe how much I look like him.

He nods. "I understand."

We eat breakfast and then pack, stuffing the trucks with supplies needed for the journey ahead. I see my dad lift up various items: canned food, blankets, flashlights, all essentials for survival in the wilderness. Lila busily stows away our personal belongings.

"Got everything?" Dad asks, his eyes scrutinizing the packed trucks.

"Yeah," I reply, my grip tightening on the strap of my bag.

"Good. Let's hit the road then," Dad declares, a determined glint in his eyes.

As we're about to climb into the trucks, a man steps out from the trees. I recognize him immediately. An ex-inmate who'd shared the same cell as me for a few years. Freddy. He'd been a friend inside and I'd mentioned this place to him, but the problem with convicts is they act on impulse and greed. Friendship means nothing if money is involved. I know it first hand. His eyes dart nervously around, landing finally on me. He brandishes a gun, pointing it straight at me.

"There's a $50,000 bounty on your head, Ash! Dead or alive," he shouts. His voice is laced with desperation, eyes glittering with the prospect of the reward.

I crack my neck. "Is that right? And how exactly are you going to kill me, Freddy?"

He waves the gun around. "How the fuck do you think?"

Suddenly, there's movement in my peripheral vision. Dad lunges at Freddy from the side, trying to grab the gun. There's a deafening bang. My heart lurches as Dad crumples to the ground, clutching his leg.

"Fucking hell!" Freddy yelps, taking a step back, his eyes wide with shock. But there's no regret in his gaze, only fear.

"Shit!" I growl, rushing to his side despite still being fucking pissed with him. His face is pale, starkly contrasting the blossoming red stain on his jeans.

"Get the gun," he gasps, his hand gripping my arm.

His other hand is on his leg, trying to stem the blood flow.

I glance back at Freddy, his face contorted with fear and uncertainty. I've seen that look before. It's the look of a cornered animal, desperate and dangerous.

I glance at Lila who is unprotected, and the sight fuels my adrenaline. Without giving it a second thought, I lunge at Freddy, tackling him to the floor. The gun skitters away from his grasp, and I deliver punch after punch.

My anger finds release on his face. He struggles beneath me, but the fight drains out of him, his body going limp. I don't stop. My fists continue to land on him even when he's no longer breathing.

"Ash! Stop!" Lila yells, her horrified voice piercing through my frenzied rage.

But I can't, I can't stop. Not yet.

A hand lands on my arm, its grip firm yet gentle. Lila. I look at her through my rage-filled haze, seeing the fear in her eyes. Her voice, a whisper now, cuts through the cloud of fury. "Stop, Ash, he's gone."

The reality of her words sinks in like a cold blade, ripping me from my rage-induced stupor. I release Freddy's lifeless body. This is who I am. Anyone who comes at me dies. Surely she realizes that by now?

Lila's gaze shifts beyond me to my dad, concern etching deeper into her features. "Ash," her voice trembles, "Your dad is losing too much blood. He needs a hospital."

Hospitals are out of the question. "I'll have to try and patch his leg up here." I walk over to him. "Can you hop if we support you?"

He nods, wincing slightly. "Yeah."

With a gentle touch, Lila moves to assist my dad. She slips an arm around his waist. I mirror her on his other side, and we guide him back to the cabin together.

His face is pale, and beads of sweat gather on his forehead as he bites back a groan.

The journey is slow and torturous, but finally, we manage to gently lower him onto the worn-out cushions of the sofa. His life hangs in the balance, and every second counts. And I'm surprised I even care.

I rummage through the dilapidated cabinets for medical supplies. I find an old, yet sealed, first aid kit. I lay out the contents. Dad's pants are soaked with blood, and as I cut away the fabric, the severity of his wound becomes apparent—it's worse than I thought.

Lila's presence is calming, her hands steady as she passes him a whiskey flask. "Here, this might help with the pain," she says softly.

Dad takes a hefty swig, his face contorting, but he nods in gratitude.

I cleanse the wound with clean water; Dad's body jerks, but he doesn't cry out. "This is going to hurt," I warn as I brace myself to do what must be done. And then I grab an old throw cushion. "Bite down on this, got it?"

He meets my gaze and nods.

I dig out the bullet with precision and speed. Dad clamps down on the throw cushion, filling the room with a muffled groan. Finally, the bullet clinks against the floor, and it's out.

Stitching is crude but necessary. I thread the needle with steady hands and stitch him up with uneven sutures. Blood seeps, but the flow lessens with each loop pulled tight.

Lila whispers words of encouragement, her voice a soothing counterpoint to his heavy breaths. It's done. I bandage the wound as best as I can, hoping it holds, hoping it's enough to keep him alive.

As I sit back on my heels, the adrenaline starts to fade, and exhaustion takes over. I look at the man lying before me. This stranger is my father.

I can't help but wonder why my hands didn't shake, why I cared enough to save a man who's been more of an absence than a presence in my life. But then I realize that blood runs thicker than resentments. Somehow, despite all the years lost, I can't let him go like this.

"We're not safe here," I state, rubbing a hand across my neck. "We'll have to shift everything into one truck and drive together."

Lila clears her throat. "I could drive one of the trucks," she suggests.

I shake my head. "It's out of the question."

She glares at me and puts her hands on her hips. "Why? Because I'm a woman."

I step toward her, pulling her close. "No, starlight

because the distance between the trucks is too fucking vast. I need you by my side."

"That's ridiculous. We need the two trucks in case one breaks down," Lila fires back, her gaze locked on mine with fierce determination. She's right, of course. I rub the bridge of my nose.

I tighten my grip on her, the words catching in my throat. "I can't breathe when you're not close," I admit, the raw truth of it spilling out uncontested. It's a vulnerability I didn't know I could voice.

Lila's eyes soften, and it's as if the world falls away. "We'll be close, in convoy the entire time."

I clench my jaw. "That's not close enough to touch you, is it?"

Her lips part. "Ash, you're acting crazy," she whispers, her voice like the brush of leaves in a hushed forest, but it cuts through the tension.

I graze my thumb over her cheek, and my voice drops to a growl. "Maybe I am, but it's better to be crazy than to lose you. The world's gone to hell. Out there," I gesture with a nod toward the woods beyond our hideout, "it's every savage for themselves, and I won't gamble with your safety."

She reaches up, her hand steady as it cradles mine, lowering it from her face. "And I won't let you smother me with your madness. I can handle myself, and you need to trust that. I'm not a damsel in distress."

I scoff, admiration swirling within me. "Listen, I'm not..." I trail off, searching her determined expression.

"Alright," I relent, my voice tight, "but we use the radios, non-stop contact, and at the first sign of trouble, we ditch a truck and converge. I mean it, first damn sign."

"Agreed," Lila says, glancing at my dad.

He nods his agreement, the worry lines etched deep in his face. He knows this world better than us, the world where the thin veneer of civilization has cracked. "Get me into my truck, and Lila can drive it. I'll direct her, and you can follow." He pulls a piece of paper from his pocket and passes it to me. "These are the coordinates just in case we get separated."

I take the paper and put it in my jacket pocket. And then we ease him up and help him limp back out of the cabin and into the passenger's side of his truck. Once the door is shut, I pull Lila out of view and against the wall of the truck, pressing her to it. "Be careful, starlight."

Her eyes meet mine with a fierceness. "Always am," she whispers back, the hint of a smile on her lips. She turns her head, kissing my cheek quickly before stepping away.

I reach out, grabbing her arm and yanking her back before she can slip away. Our bodies collide, and without a second thought, my hands cradle her face, pulling her into a hard and deep kiss fueled by a storm of emotions I've barely kept at bay. When I finally break away, I can't help but growl the promise that's been burning within me, "You're mine, Lila, now and forever."

She looks into my eyes and nods. "Yours. We should get going."

As I look at her, I know I love her with all my heart. A crazy, all-consuming love that drives me mad.

Stepping back, I watch her climb into the truck, gripping the wheel with those delicate hands. Dad already looks more at ease.

I shake off the swarm of butterflies caged in my chest and head to the other truck.

I fire up the engine, the rumble a familiar comfort in these unsettling times. Glancing in the rearview mirror, I catch a last glimpse of the fading security of Dad's cabin, a once haven now vulnerable.

I won't be at ease until we're safely in Alaska, I think to myself, gripping the steering wheel until my knuckles turn white. Crossing the border to Canada is treacherous, but it's the only path to a real future with my starlight. It's a risk we've got to take. With every mile we move away from the cabin, we're one step closer to salvation—or so I hope.

20

LILA

The sky has begun to bruise with the purples and blues of twilight as the truck crunches over the gravel road. Every thrum of the engine is a step further into the unknown.

Gone is the Lila that once clung to rules and the safety of the familiar. Trees blur into a monochrome dance as the wilderness envelops us. The road ahead is a murky, uncharted path, but I'm ready to chase the Northern lights to freedom with every fiber of my being.

The unruly wilderness of Canada looms ahead, a guardian of the threshold that separates my old life from the new. Tonight, we'll brave it, paperwork be damned. Tonight, I trust in the wild and the raw love that propels me forward into a life that's mine to shape.

I glance in the rearview mirror to see Ash's truck close behind.

"Take it steady here. We're close to the border," Ash's

dad, Liam, grunts. His face is still ghostly pale after he got shot, and the bumps on this track are punishing on his wound.

"I will," I breathe, biting my lip. "How many times have you successfully crossed over this border?"

"Two times, this is my third attempt."

That's not many times, but I don't voice my doubts. I try to remain positive, hoping we make it over. The last thing we need is to have come all this way to stumble at the last hurdle.

The dusky sky is now streaked with the last hints of day. I tighten my grip on the steering wheel, willing my nerves to steady as we inch closer to the invisible line that cuts through the wilderness – a border unseen but heavily felt.

Ash's voice crackles through the walkie-talkie. "Remember, if anyone stops us, we're out for a late-night drive, got lost from the main road," he reminds me.

I nod to myself. "Promise me we'll make it," I whisper into the walkie-talkie.

"Promise," comes the reply, near-instant and certain.

Suddenly, red and blue lights slice through the shroud of darkness ahead, a stark warning that shatters the silent tension. I pull over before the cop car, heart thundering, as an officer steps out of the patrol car with cautious strides, a hand resting near his holster. "Are you folks alright?" he asks, his beam of light scanning the area, systematically stripping away our veneer of calm.

I can barely find my words. "We lost the main road," I lie.

The officer shifts, attention snapping behind us. "Is that truck with you?" he asks, voice rising with a clear edge of alarm.

"Yes, we were out for a drive and got lost."

He notices the bandage on Liam's leg and the blood stain. "I'm going to have to ask both of you to exit your vehicle now." He pulls his gun, aiming it at us.

I hold my hands up. "Of course, officer. No problem."

Liam pulls the gun he's hidden beneath the dash as he fumbles to get out, limping around.

My heart is hammering so hard I think I'm going to pass out any minute.

Before I can so much as gasp, a gunshot pierces the night, the sound resonating through the once-tranquil forest. Time slows, and the stars above witness the chaos below.

Liam stumbles as he tries to shoot the officer. The officer is too quick and returns fire, the bullet finding its home in his chest. He collapses with a thud that seems to silence the world.

Ash leaps from the other truck, moving with reckless fury, the barrel of his gun pointed at the officer. A sharp shot shatters the fraught silence, and the officer crumples to the forest floor, a life extinguished in the blink of an eye.

He sprints to his dad's side. "Fuck!" he bellows, falling

to his knees and placing a hand over the bleeding wound in his chest. "There's no patching that up," he murmurs.

Liam nods, jaw clenching. "It's okay," he mutters, shaking his head. "At least you can get out of here. You're almost there."

Ash watches as his dad's breaths are shallow and ragged. There's little emotion detectable in his eyes. After all, he doesn't really know the man before him.

"Ash," Liam chokes out. "I'm sorry for everything," he gasps, his hand feebly searching for Ash's. "I wasn't there, but I..."

With bitterness in his eyes and a quiver in his lip, Ash seems locked in a tumultuous inner battle as he holds his father's gaze. It's a dance of anger and yearning. The final moments of a bond that could've been urging them toward an unreachable peace.

Ash's fingers entwine with Liam's, the grip far from the tender clasp of familial affection. It's the clasp of a son betrayed. "Save your breath," he says through clenched teeth.

His father's eyes plead for the mercy of absolution.

"You missed your chance," Ash spits out, the words cutting through the silence sharper than the cold air against their skin.

The man before him coughs, pleading at him with his eyes. But the chasm between them is too vast, the years too heavy, the anger too deep. Liam's last breath is heavy, laden with unsaid words and apologies that came too late.

And my heart aches for them both. It's a tragedy for Ash to lose his father so soon after finding out he's still alive and for his father, who dies, never getting the forgiveness he craved from his son.

But perhaps, in their final moments together, there's a glimmer of understanding. And maybe, just maybe, this can be the start of the healing process for Ash to help him move forward from a life full of darkness and destruction.

*a*chill wind sweeps through the woods, tousling my hair as I stand over the freshly turned earth. I lean on the shovel, the tool now an extension of the darkness growing within me. Beside me, Lila trembles, whether from cold or emotion, I can't tell.

We stand under the waning moonlight. My father is buried beneath the earth. All I feel is anger. A cold ember that glows within the darkness I embody. There's no room for the luxury of sorrow or the softness of grief. My mind is wired differently, programmed to prioritize survival over sentiment.

"I'm sorry," Lila whispers, breaking the silence.

I turn to look at her. "Save it," I reply, my voice devoid of warmth.

Lila bristles but says nothing more, and I can see the confusion and conflict dancing in her vibrant blue eyes. I'm all too aware of what her agreeing to come with me means. She's mine forever, and that's what I want, but I don't deserve it. She deserves a man better than me.

Lila's presence is a constant source of unwanted emotion, carving fissures in my resolve and in the walls I built to keep such distractions at bay.

Lila's hand reaches for mine.

I pull away as if scorched by the air she breathes. I've been out of control since the day I forced her to come with me on the side of the road.

Fuck.

I even let her tattoo her name over my heart. When did she slip through the walls around my heart, and why in God's name did I let her?

"You can't keep doing this," Lila's voice cuts through the thick tension. "Stop pulling away," she breathes out, every word dripping with a raw, desperate hunger, seeking to claim something from the depths of my soul.

I feel it, the relentless pull of her presence, like the inevitable draw of a ravenous flame. "Why?" My voice is a low growl. "Tell me why I should let you in when all you'll find is darkness?"

Her hand finds its way to my chest over the unseen mark of her name. "Because underneath all that fury, that pain you wield like a weapon," she whispers, "there's a heart that beats with the same ferocity with which you push the world away. Let me in. Even the darkness needs its starlight, right?"

Her words are a cruel echo of my own, gnawing at the defenses of my hardened heart.

She's my starlight. And starlight deserves to be cherished. I fear I can't give her what she deserves. "I'm bad for you. You should take the other truck and drive home."

Tears flood her eyes. "You don't get to decide what's bad for me," she says. "You were the one who convinced me to come with you, and now things are hard you want to toss me aside, is that it?"

"Tossing you aside? I'm allowing you to be free of my darkness. Of a darkness that'll destroy you in the end."

"And what happened to me being a permanent part of your life? Did you forget what you said?" She demands, glaring at me through tear filled eyes. "You're mine, and you're never going to escape."

I clench my jaw because I did say that. Since we met, I've been spiraling off the deep end, forgetting the most important rule. Trust no one. Never let anyone in. And yet here we are.

"I meant it, but what life can I give you in Alaska?"

She steps closer, nostrils flaring. "The life I want. I'll run my blog. Screw my job back home and live side by side with you, keeping in check your darkness." She tilts her head. "You know, I was worried that I was only drawn to you because of my past." She shakes her head. "I know now that's not true. It's because we're fated to be together. You're my redemption, and I'm yours."

"Dammit, Lila," I roar. "Why do you have to make this so fucking difficult?"

She doesn't recoil. "I don't think I'm the one making

things difficult. We've come this far. Let's keep going. Together."

I grab her hips, forcing her against me. "Fuck, starlight." I kiss her passionately, allowing those walls to fall away. "I fucking love you."

Lila tenses, and I wonder if I've said it too soon. She won't say it back, but it's the truth. Ever since I looked into her eyes on the side of the road, I knew my life as I knew it was over.

"I don't know what to say." Her fingers tentatively trace my jaw. The proximity of her breath, laced with the scent of rose, is a balm to the storm within me.

"You don't have to say anything," I murmur. "You're here *with* me – that's all I need." I press my forehead against hers. The cool Canadian wilderness is forgotten, replaced by the fire between us. Darkness threads through my veins, a living thing that's found its counterpart in her light.

She swallows hard. "I'm not afraid of your darkness," Lila declares, her voice breaking through my brooding silence. "I never was."

With a growl of possession, I haul her back into the truck. Every click and slide of the seats folding down echoes like a drumbeat. "Get in," I command.

"But, I—"

"Ssh," I silence her with a finger pressed to her lips. "Get in, lie down, and take your panties off."

Her eyes dilate, and she does as she's told, swiftly lying down and pulling her panties off. My eyes drink her in, and the suppressed beast within approves. And then I climb inside with her, feeling the ring in my cock grazing against the fabric as I get harder.

I liberate myself from the confines of fabric, my cock aching. Each deliberate stroke, amplified by my piercings, making me groan."Spread your legs for me," I command. Every shred of moonlight illuminates her obedience as she parts them slowly. "That's it, starlight, let me see all of you. Laid bare and offered up to me." My gaze devours the sight of her soaking wet cunt glistening and ready.

"Are you going to fuck me?"

I smirk. "I'm going to destroy you. Don't say I didn't warn you."

She bites her lip. "Can you put the mask on?"

"Fuck, you're so dirty, baby." I grab her throat and squeeze. "Do you want me to pretend I'm a stranger again?"

Her voice comes out in a breathy dare, "Yes, I want you to take me like you're stealing every breath, every moan."

I respond, a cruel twist at the corner of my mouth, "You want the rush, huh? That fear-spiked thrill?" I slide the mask over my face, the darkness clinging to me like a second skin. "I'll give you the high that'll haunt your dreams."

With the mask on, my world narrows to her and the hunger that claws at me from the inside. My hands, hard and unyielding, grip her thighs, pulling them apart further. "Like this," I growl, "So I can watch you unravel."

"Stop!" she cries out, naturally falling into her role.

Her whimper fuels my dominance. "Telling me to stop only makes my dick harder," I snarl.

There's a flash in her eyes as if I'm challenging her. "Stop this! I don't want it." She pushes against me with her hand, and I grab it with mine, forcing it over her head.

"Liar," I growl, resting the head of my throbbing dick at her entrance, allowing the ring to rub gently against her clit. "I see how much you want my cock in your eyes."

She bites her lip to stop herself from crying out. "No, don't do it."

I smirk at her, my cock leaking precum onto her cunt. My eyes holding hers through the holes in my mask as I slam into her with enough force to leave her breathless, "There's nothing in this world that could stop me from fucking what belongs to me," I breathe into her ear, keeping her hands restrained above her head. "I can't get enough."

My starlight spread wide, impaled, and gasping is a heavenly sight. Her body arches against mine, the lie on her lips apparent in the desperate way her hips buck to meet my thrusts.

I watch her through the holes in my mask, relishing how the moonlight floods the windows and casts shadows across her perfect features. Her eyes dart around, searching for an escape that doesn't exist.

When I strike a particularly sensitive spot, her soft moans and the sharp intake of breath are all music to my ears.

"Fuck, Ash, please don't," she gasps, a sob punctuating her words.

I grin behind the mask, relishing her futile resistance. "I thought you liked it rough, starlight," I purr, pushing into her even harder, my cock finding its home deep.

She tries to push me away, her hands still trapped above her head. "No! Stop it, I told you to stop."

But I don't stop. I can't stop. Lila doesn't want me to stop because she'd use our safe word if she did. My dick throbs inside her, aching to spill my cum.

"Open your mouth, starlight," I command, needing to taste her again.

She shakes her head violently. "No!"

I grab her jaw, forcing her mouth open, and then I take her, my tongue delving into the depths of her mouth. I want to consume her, to make her mine in every way.

Her hands finally go limp, her body surrendering to the inevitable. She moans again, the sounds of her pleasure filling the air.

"That's it," I growl, thrusting into her even harder. "Submit to me."

She tries to hold back, but it's no use. She moans, her eyes so dilated they look like pure black coals.

"Say it," I growl, thrusting harder. "Say that you want me to fuck you."

"Fuck me," she whispers, voice hoarse. "Fill me up."

I give her what she wants, a relentless onslaught that leaves no room for breath or thought. Her body bucks beneath me, her nails digging into my back. Her moans are music to my ears, a symphony of surrender.

"You feel so good," I groan, my words barely audible above the sounds of our primal fucking. "So tight and wet. I want you to come for me, baby. Let me see you come."

Her climax wracks her body in violent waves. I watch, mesmerized, as her eyes roll back in her head.

With a final, shuddering thrust, I reach my peak, spilling my cum deep inside her. The tension in my body melts away, replaced by a sense of satisfaction.

For a moment, we lie still, our bodies slick with sweat. I can feel her heart pounding against my chest, a rapid, erratic beat that mirrors my own.

"That was..." She trails off, searching for words. "That was amazing, but Ash—"

"No," I cut her off, rolling away from her. "Don't ruin it."

She frowns. "Ruin what?"

"The moment," I growl. "Don't talk about what happened."

Lila sighs. "I don't understand."

"What's there to understand?" I snap.

"We need to talk about what happened to your—"

"Don't say it." My fingers clench into fists. Talk? What is there to talk about? I met my dad for the first time since I was born. He got shot, and we buried him. End of fucking story.

"There's nothing to talk about," I say.

She sighs but accepts that I'm not ready. I may never be ready. "Fine. What happens now?"

My heart hammers in my chest. What happens now? Two people whose lives have become irrevocably intertwined. Two people bound together by desire and circumstance.

"You're mine, and I'm yours; it's that simple," I finally say. I reach out and take Lila's hand, interlocking our fingers. "We'll figure this out," I promise.

There's a mixture of hope and uncertainty in her eyes. "I hope you're right."

We lie down again, facing each other. Lila's eyes are clear and unguarded, reflecting the tumultuous journey we've been on.

"I love you, Lila," I whisper, the words tumbling out of my mouth again before I can stop them.

Her eyes widen. She shakes her head. "Ash, I don't—"

I press a finger to her lips. "Don't say anything, starlight. It might take you longer to get there, but you will."

The bold words roll off my tongue with an air of finality, a declaration of ownership that leaves no room for argument.

I lean in, closing the distance between us. Her eyes, those captivating pools of sapphire, shimmer under the pale moonlight that filters through the window.

"You're mine," I repeat, my breath ghosting across her cheek. "And I'm yours."

I press my lips against hers, a soft, tentative kiss gradually deepening. Our tongues dance a sensual tango that speaks of our undeniable connection.

I feel her surrender in the way her body molds against mine, in the way her fingers tighten on my shirt.

"I can't promise you it'll be easy," I continue, "but I can promise you this - you'll never experience anything like it. You're meant for this, Lila. Meant to be with me."

Lila is my starlight, piercing through the darkness and illuminating my soul.

"You really believe that?" she asks, her voice barely a whisper.

I nod, my gaze unwavering. "I do."

She leans in and kisses me again. Her fingers tangle in my hair, pulling me closer. Time stands still as we lose ourselves in the kiss, the world around us fading into insignificance.

For the first time, I feel like I've found a home. Finally, we pull apart and dress silently before continuing our perilous journey.

A sense of unease lingers as I revel in the newfound closeness. The shadows of my pasts still loom, threatening to consume both of us. The road ahead is fraught with uncertainty.

Can I truly escape the darkness that lurks within me? Or are we both destined to be consumed by it?

22

ASH

*T*he tires crunch on the gravel as the car pulls to a stop, dust settling around us like a shroud. We've been on the road for days, the horizon stretching before us. The anticipation, a quiet hum beneath my skin, finally comes to a head as I stare at the place my father built.

It stands there, a haven amid the wilderness. There's a larger log-built chalet and a smaller cabin, as Dad described. It's picturesque and nestled beside a sprawling lake, surrounded by a silent congregation of trees.

The isolation of this place is perfect for our escape; a part of me wishes he were here. A part of me is relieved I don't have to deal with the wounds of my past.

Lila sits beside me, her gaze tracing the landscape with awe and trepidation. She's my prize, and it's almost poetic that I have her with me after the chaos I've left behind. The road we took was painted with sins, each mile marker a testament to my actions. I'm a convicted murderer, a man with blood on his hands, and this paradise is the antithesis of what I deserve.

But standing here, looking at the tranquility I can't help but feel a sense of twisted accomplishment. The lake mirrors the calm surface I try to present, while the trees, their branches intertwined, remind me of the dark thoughts that coil around my conscience.

The wind whispers through the leaves, carrying the scent of pine with it. I should be haunted by the lives I've taken, but there's a numbness instead. It's the only way I've learned to cope—with detachment.

The chalet looms before us, its doors welcoming. As we step out of the truck, the reality of our newfound refuge settles over us like a shroud. Dad's home is now mine, a sanctuary tainted by the shadows I've brought with me.

"How are you feeling?" Lila asks pity in her pretty blue eyes.

I hate her pity.

"I'm fine," I lie, shrugging off her concern.

Lila's gaze narrows, slicing through my defenses with an intensity that sets my blood on fire. She sees through the facade and recognizes the damaged soul behind the mask.

"Fine?" she asks.

"Let's go inside," I murmur, ignoring her question.

I reach for her hand, her skin against mine an anchor.

We move toward the chalet, our steps synchronized on the gravel path.

I slide the key into the intricately carved front door before pushing it open to reveal a grand foyer bathed in the warm glow of the setting sun that spills through the tall windows. The light dances across polished wooden floors, and the scent of aged mahogany fills the air.

"This is breathtaking," Lila whispers, her voice carrying a note of awe.

I nod, feeling the tightness in my chest ease while I watch her marvel at the beauty around us.

The concept of love, that illusion peddled by poets and fools, had always been foreign to me. My heart, a fortress of solitude, impenetrable and cold—never had it quickened for another.

Desire? Yes. Lust? Undeniably. But love had never tempted me to abandon the embrace of darkness until Lila came with piercing eyes and auburn curls and challenged the void where my heart should beat.

My boots thud against the wooden floor as we walk through the grand foyer. The walls are adorned with antlers and mounted animal heads.

A sweeping staircase with an intricate wrought-iron railing to my right beckons us upward. A massive stone fireplace dominates the living room, its hearth cold.

Lila's hand tightens in mine, her grip a lifeline in this sea of unfamiliar opulence.

As we pass through the living room, my gaze falls upon the grand piano in the corner. Its polished, ebony surface reflects the flickering firelight, inviting me to touch its keys. My mom may have been a drug addict, but I remember she used to play so beautifully on an old worn out piano to get me to sleep.

I tear my eyes away from the piano and continue toward the kitchen, the scent of pine and cedarwood lingering in the air. The kitchen is spacious, with a large center island and state-of-the-art appliances. It's a far cry from the cramped little log cabin we left behind. We're a world away from my past.

Lila releases my hand and walks to the window, her forehead pressed against the cool glass. The sun has set outside, casting the surrounding forest in an inky abyss. The only light source comes from the moon, its pale glow illuminating the snow-covered peaks of the distant mountains. It's a breathtaking sight, one that soothes the restlessness within me.

"It's beautiful," Lila murmurs.

I stand beside her, my gaze drawn to the moonlit landscape. It's a scene of peace and tranquility.

"Yes, it is," I agree.

We stand there in silence, the moonlight casting long shadows across the kitchen.

A desire, raw and primal, surges through me. I want to taste Lila, to feel her beneath me, to lose myself in the oblivion of her body.

It's like wildfire, consuming my entire being. I can't deny the primal urge that grips me, the need to possess her, to make her mine in every sense of the word.

I turn to face her, my gaze devouring her. Her eyes widen in surprise, her lips parting in anticipation. I reach out and cup her cheek, the softness of her skin sending shivers down my spine. I watch her closely, my heart pounding in my chest.

"Get on your knees," I demand.

Lila doesn't hesitate. She quickly drops to her knees before me. She looks at me with a mixture of fear and desire in her eyes.

I reach out and grab her hair, pulling it back sharply. Her gasp echoes through the room as I tighten my grip. "You know what you are," I growl, my voice rising as I pull harder. "My dirty little slut."

Lila's body trembles as she nods, acknowledging the truth of my words. She is a slut, a dirty little thing who belongs to me.

My piercings tug at my dick as my cock gets so hard it drives me crazy. I watch Lila's reaction to my dominance as she squirms, rubbing her thighs together.

"I'm going to fuck your throat," I tell her.

Lila licks her lips before opening her mouth, her eyes filled with lust and submission.

"Good girl," I whisper, pulling my cock out of my pants and thrusting it into her throat.

She gags instantly, the size too much for her to take.

I'm not sure what it is about her, but something about this girl makes me want to be better for her. I can't help but dominate her, though, making her submit to my will. It's intoxicating.

Her eyes glisten with tears as she struggles to keep up with the intensity of my thrusts. I pull back, watching as her lips part and her tongue lap eagerly at the pierced head of my cock.

As I pull my cock from Lila's throat, she gasps for air, her eyes wide. I don't give her time to catch her breath before I grab her by the arm and force her to her feet.

"What are you doing?"

I growl against her ear. "No questions."

I bend her face first over the kitchen table, my hand gripping the back of her head as I force her down onto the cold wooden surface. Her body trembles beneath me as I rip off her panties, tearing them into shreds with my fingers.

"You want me inside you, don't you?" I whisper in her ear, my breath hot against her skin.

My hands roam over her bare ass, squeezing and kneading the flesh as she whimpers beneath me. Her hips buck forward, seeking contact with the edge of the table.

"Yes," she moans.

"Say it," I demand. "Tell me how much you need me to fuck you."

My fingers slide lower, tracing the edges of her pussy lips before dipping inside.

She cries out, her body arching off the table as I tease her. "I need you to fuck me so badly."

"Good girl," I praise her, pushing two fingers deep inside her wet heat. She clenches around me, her walls contracting as she tries to draw me further in.

With a grunt, I pull back and line up my cock with her entrance. With one powerful thrust, I drive myself all the way inside her, making her cry out in surprise and pleasure. Her nails dig into the wood surface as I begin to pound into her mercilessly, my hips slapping against her ass with each stroke.

"You're so tight," I growl, my voice low and menacing as I fuck her deeper and deeper. "So fucking tight."

"Oh, fuck!" she cries.

"You like this, don't you? You love being used like a filthy little whore."

She moans louder as we fuck, the sound of our bodies colliding echoing through the room.

My cock slams into her over and over again, each impact sending shockwaves of pleasure coursing through her body.

"Ash!" She screams out my name, lost in the sensation of being filled to the brim by me.

Reaching around, I grab hold of one of her breasts, squeezing and tweaking her nipple between my fingers. Her back arches as my cock sinks deeper.

I play with her clit, circling it with my fingers until she can't take it anymore. Her body convulses as she climaxes hard, sending waves of pleasure coursing through us both.

Once she climaxes, I pump my cum into her pussy until it spills out onto the kitchen table below. She moans louder still as we continue fucking, our bodies moving in perfect harmony together.

As she comes down from her high, I pull out of her pussy and watch as more of my cum drips out onto the kitchen table. It's a sight to behold, my cum spilling out onto the cold wooden surface in a steady stream.

"I'm going to pump your ass full," I tell her, my voice low.

She moans at the thought of being filled up by me again, making my semi-hard cock instantly solid again.

I grab the bottle of olive oil on the counter with one hand. With the other hand, I grab Lila by the hips and pull her to the edge of the table. Spreading it onto my fingers, I use them to stretch her ass open.

Her body tenses as I push them inside, but she relaxes quickly once they're in place.

I watch as she takes my fingers, feeling them stretch her open before I start pumping them in and out of her ass. Her moans grow louder as I stretch her ass until it's gaping and ready for my cock.

I tug on my already hard cock and position it against her puckered hole. She moans at the feel of my cock against her skin, feeling its weight press down on her.

"I'm going to fuck your ass so hard you'll beg for mercy, and when you do, I'll fill it with cum."

She moans, arching her back in invitation. "Ash," she breathes my name.

With a deep breath, I slowly push forward, inch by inch, until I'm buried inside her. She gasps in pain as I slowly move in and out of her ass. As I continue to thrust into her, I grab onto her hips, holding her close.

"You like being a dirty little slut, don't you?" I ask her, my voice rough with desire. "You love having my big cock up your ass, feeling it stretch you open and fill you up."

"Yes, fuck me harder." She glances at me over her shoulder. "Talk dirty to me."

I smirk at her request, leaning closer and whispering directly into her ear. "You know what I'm going to do, right? I'm going to make you my little anal slut. You're going to take everything I give you without complaint. And when I'm done, you'll be so fucked up that you won't be able to walk straight."

Instead of backing away, she pushes back against me, taking more of my cock inside her.

With that, I redouble my efforts, pounding into her with a ferocity that leaves her gasping for air. My hands move to her breasts, squeezing and pinching her nipples until they're hard and aching.

"You like that, don't you? You love being used like a piece of meat," I growl. "You're nothing but a hole for me to fuck, and you wouldn't have it any other way."

Her moans become louder, more desperate, as she clings to the table for dear life. She's completely lost in the sensations, unable to form coherent thoughts beyond begging for more.

"Say it," I demand, pulling out and turning her around to face me. "Tell me what you are."

"I'm your dirty slut," she gasps, her cheeks flushed with embarrassment and arousal.

"That's right," I praise her, forcing her back onto the kitchen table but facing me and then slamming back inside her.

I grab her hips roughly, using them as leverage to drive myself deeper into her. My movements become more erratic, more primal, as I lose myself in the pleasure of claiming her body.

"You're mine," I snarl, biting down on her shoulder hard enough to leave a mark. "You belong to me, and no one else will ever touch you like this."

She screams out in pain and pleasure, her legs trembling. I can feel her orgasm building within her, and I know that I won't last much longer, either.

"That's it, baby. Come on my cock."

Her pussy clenches around me like a vice as she tumbles over the edge. "Yes! Fuck! Yes!"

With a final, brutal thrust, I empty myself inside her, filling her up with my cum. I pull out and look at the wonderful image of her spread wide, pussy dripping my cum still, and her ass gaping as she pushes my cum out of it. "I've never seen anything so fucking beautiful," I murmur. I take a photo on my cell phone to add to the collection and then pull her off the table, cradling her in my arms.

She rests her head against my chest, her breathing ragged. I run my fingers through her hair, savoring the feel of her soft curls against my skin. And then I set her gently on the floor.

I take her hand and lead her to the window, where the

stars shine brightly. "Look at these stars," I tell her. "They're like diamonds scattered across the sky. And just like these diamonds, you're my most precious possession."

She turns to face me, her eyes shining with tears. "Ash, I still don't—"

"Ssh, starlight. If you can't find the words, say nothing." I grind my teeth. "I already know you'll feel it someday." I smile at her and lean closer, pressing my lips against hers. "You're my everything," I declare.

She steps closer to me, wrapping her arms around me tightly. Lila has changed me in ways I never thought possible. She's shown me there's more to life than violence. She's given me hope for a future I never dreamed of.

I hold her close, feeling the weight of the world lifted from my shoulders. In this moment, everything feels right. I'm exactly where I'm supposed to be with the woman I love. Lifting her, I carry her up the stairs and into a bedroom, placing her gently on the bed. And then we lie there for a long time in silence, basking in each other.

Eventually, Lila stirs in my arms. She looks at me, her eyes sparkling with what I could only describe as love.

"I never want this to end," she whispers.

"Me neither," I say, pulling her close again. "I want to be with you forever."

We kiss, a slow, lingering kiss that promises a lifetime

of love and happiness. When we finally pull away, we're both breathless.

I feel truly happy for the first time in my life. I've found love, and I've found a home.

Lila and I will build a new life in this beautiful place. We'll grow old together happily, neither thing I believed possible for me until I stumbled upon her on the side of that road.

23
EPILOGUE

LILA

*O*ne year later...

Ash sits at the river's edge with his fishing rod, gazing over the sparkling water as the sun's rays catch it. He looks almost angelic. Although he's quite possibly the furthest thing from an angel on this earth.

He's a devil. A beast. A monster.

But I love him despite it all.

We've settled naturally into our life here, and I've noticed a shift in Ash. His anger seems to ebb away when he's surrounded by the peace and quiet of Alaska. I've even managed to convince him to quit smoking, for the most part. On occasion, I've come home from town to find him with one between his lips. He says it's because it's the only way for him to feel sane when I'm so far from him.

Despite the remoteness of our Alaskan haven, I've managed to carve out a digital corner with my blog, which has flourished. The only hitch is the inconsistent internet connectivity in our chalet, compelling me to drive thirty minutes to the nearest town whenever I need to upload new content. But the drive, often accompanied by the crisp air and scenic tapestry of wilderness, has become a ritual I've come to enjoy, a small price to pay for the tranquility that feeds my writing.

Not to mention, I've made a few friends my age in town. Ash likes to stay away from people, though. He rarely accompanies me. He fears that mingling with the rest of society could risk everything he's running from. He believes his impulse control isn't fixed and that one argument with someone could make him snap and murder again. I'm not so sure.

I know that he's unhinged and borderline psychotic, and I've questioned how I can love a man like him. A man so savage and violent, but it just works. He fits me like a glove, and I wouldn't change him for the world, no matter how unconventional our meeting.

My parents were supportive of the move and apparently Brian lost his shit when he heard. My dad went to pick up all my stuff from our apartment and he almost had a fight with him. I don't care though. I'm glad I've escaped him finally.

They're going to visit at some point, but I know they're busy.

"Ash!" I call his name, and he turns, glancing at me and smiling.

"Hey, starlight! How was town?"

I move closer to him, clutching the box of donuts I bought from the town bakery.

I hand him a donut, and he groans in appreciation. "Fuck, baby. You know how to spoil me, don't you?"

"It's only a donut."

He bites into it and moans. "Almost as sweet as you," he murmurs, eyes dancing with that dark allure. I know what he's thinking already, and then I notice the way his grey jogging pants cling to his huge erection. My stomach clenches, and an ache immediately ignites between my thighs.

Ignoring it, I clear my throat. "Have you caught much?"

He smirks and nods at the nearby net holding several trout. The lake at our chalet is fed by a stream, providing a good source of free food, especially in the summer. "Yeah, we'll eat tonight, for sure."

I laugh. "I bought us steak, which I'm going to cook, but the trout will keep."

He arches a brow. "Splashing out on steak?"

"You know the blog is doing well, so why not? I fancied it."

He grabs me by the hips and pulls me onto his lap, groaning. "Okay, but first, I've got more important things that need to be tended to."

"Such as?"

"You know, my favorite game I like to play."

I bite my lip as he loves to chase me through the

woods. It's become one of our favorite things to role-play. Me the prey, him the hunter.

"Do you have a mask?" I ask.

He pulls out our new favorite ghostface mask. "Of course." He winks. "I'm always prepared."

"Okay, let's play."

He smirks and forces me off his lap, standing.

I take a deep breath, my heart racing as I look at Ash. He's standing there, his piercing gaze fixed on me. His muscles ripple as he flexes his arms, and I can't help but feel a shiver run down my spine.

"Okay," he growls, "Run for me, starlight."

My heart pounds as I turn around and rush toward the trees.

"Ten, Nine, Eight..." I hear him counting, but the faster I run, the more distant his voice grows.

The trees whiz by me as I sprint as fast as I can, my legs pumping furiously. I can hear Ash call out louder this time. "Run fast, starlight, as no one can outrun the darkness!"

I squeal softly under my breath and quicken my pace. After a few minutes, I'm breathless and panting, so I stop by a tree to regain energy and catch my breath.

After allowing myself no more than twenty seconds, I keep moving. But I hear Ash moving loudly through the woods, tracking me like an innate predator.

As I round a bend in the path, I see a small stream ahead. It's narrow and fast-moving, with rocks lining the bottom of it.

I pick up my pace, determined not to let him catch up to me. But he appears out of nowhere when I think I might be able to make it across the stream without him seeing me. He grabs my arm and pulls me back toward him with all his strength. My body is thrown off balance, and before I know it, we're both tumbling to the ground together.

I gasp for air as Ash's weight crushes me into the ground. His hands grip my arms tightly, holding me in place as he leans over me. His eyes are dark and intense, and I can feel his breath hot against my face.

"You're mine," he growls in my ear. "I own you now."

His words send a shiver down my spine, and I can feel myself getting wet as I know how rough he gets when we play this game.

"I'm going to fuck you so hard," he continues, "you won't be able to walk for days."

His words send another shiver down my spine, making my nipples harden. He's always been so domi-nant with me, and I love it.

"Please," I beg him, "don't do this."

But he just laughs at me, his grip tightening even more on my arms as he pushes himself harder against me. His cock is huge and hard, pressing through the fabric of his pants. I can feel every inch of him against me.

And then he reaches between us and pulls down his joggers, forcing his huge cock out. With his other hand, he roughly forces my skirt up to my waist, and then he groans. "Such a dirty little slut, not wearing panties," he growls, nostrils flaring. "Did you go into town like that?"

I tilt my head and shrug. "It's hot out. I like how it feels going commando."

"Well, at least you made this so much easier." He slams into me with force, tearing my pussy apart and making me moan.

He's so big and rough, and it feels so good. I can feel every inch of him stretching me out, making me wetter than I've ever been before.

"You like that, don't you?" he growls in my ear. "You like being fucked hard and rough."

I nod, unable to speak, as he continues to pound into me. My body is on fire, every nerve ending alive with pleasure. I can feel myself getting closer and closer to the edge, but I don't want it to end. Not yet.

"Tell me you're mine," he demands, his voice rough and low.

"I'm yours," I whisper, looking at him with pleading eyes.

He groans and picks me up, slamming me against a nearby tree. My back arches as he continues to thrust into me, his hips slapping against my ass. It's so dirty and wrong, but it feels so right.

"You're such a dirty little slut," he pants, his breath hot against my neck. "I'm going to make you scream for more."

And then he reaches around and starts fingering my clit, sending shockwaves of pleasure through my body. I cry out, my legs shaking as I grip onto his shoulders for support.

"That's it, baby," he murmurs, his lips brushing against my ear. "Let go, and let me take you where you need to go."

I can't hold back any longer. My orgasm crashes over me like a wave, leaving me shaking and panting. Ash follows me over the edge, groaning as he explodes inside me.

For a moment, we just remain there, him standing and me pressed against the tree, panting heavily. And then he pulls out of me and lowers me to the ground, leaving me feeling empty and wanting more.

"You're such a tease, I need more." I pout.

He chuckles and pulls me into his arms, kissing me softly. "I love how greedy you are," he murmurs. "It only makes me want you more. Although you didn't do too well at playing the victim that time, starlight. What happened?"

I bite my lip and shrug. "Sometimes it's hard to when I'm so turned on."

He laughs. "But I love it when you scream no," he breathes into my ear.

I punch him playfully. "You're such a bad man," I whisper.

He smirks and pulls me closer, nibbling on my ear. "And you love that about me, don't you?"

I nod, unable to deny the truth in his words. As much as I hate to admit it, something about how he treats me turns me on. It's dangerous and thrilling, and I can't get enough of it.

"Come on," he says, pulling me to my feet. "Let's go back to the chalet. I've got plans for you."

I shiver with anticipation, allowing him to lead me back to our chalet . I know whatever he has in store for me, it's going to be wild and passionate. And I can't wait.

Ash and I walk back to the chalet, hand in hand. The sun is setting, casting long shadows across the path. The air is cool and crisp, and I can smell the scent of pine needles.

We reach the chalet, and Ash opens the door, ushering me inside. I step through and immediately feel the warmth of the fire crackling in the fireplace.

"I've cooked us something special, so the steak will have to wait until tomorrow," Ash says, leading me into the kitchen.

I see a table set for two, with candles flickering in the center. He goes to the over and pulls out a roast chicken, mashed potatoes and vegetables, placing them on the table.

"Wow, Ash," I say, impressed. "This looks amazing."

"I wanted to do something nice for you," he says, pulling out my chair. "You deserve it after all your hard work in town."

I smile and sit down. Ash takes his seat across from me, and we begin to eat.

"So, how did it go today?" he asks.

"I finished and submitted that post I'd been working on for my blog." I shrug. "We'll see how it goes."

"I'm so glad you're doing something you love," he says when I finish. "You're so talented, starlight. You deserve all the success in the world."

I blush and look down at my plate. "Thank you," I murmur.

We continue to eat, and the conversation flows easily. Ash tells me about his day chopping wood for winter and fishing. We talk about our plans for the future, our dreams, and our aspirations. I'd never felt so hopeful for the future until I met this man.

After eating, Ash clears the table and brings two glasses of wine. He hands me one, and we sit on the couch before the fire.

We sip our wine and talk longer about nothing in particular. Just enjoying each other's company.

Eventually, Ash takes my hand and looks into my eyes.

"Lila," he says, his voice low and husky, "I've got something to ask you."

My heart starts to race. "What is it?"

He drops to one knee before me and it feels like my world is spinning. And then he pulls out a stunning vintage engagement ring with a huge sapphire in the center. "Will you marry me?"

I stare at him for a moment, stunned. Tears well up in my eyes. "Yes," I say, my voice trembling. "Yes, Ash, I'll marry you."

He smiles and pushes the ring onto my finger before pulling me into his arms. I can feel his heart beating against my chest.

"I love you so much," he whispers. "I can't imagine my life without you."

"I love you too," I say. "More than anything in the world."

We kiss, and it's a kiss full of love and passion. I feel like I'm melting into him. When we finally pull away, Ash rests his forehead against mine.

"I promise to love you forever," he says. "I promise to protect you and make you happy."

I believe him. I know that he will.

We sit there for a long time, holding each other and enjoying the moment. I feel like I'm the luckiest woman in the world.

I've found my soulmate in the most fucked up and unconventional way. And I know I'll spend the rest of my life with him. It's hard to believe something so beautiful blossomed from one of the darkest experiences of my life.

I can't wait to continue our new life together.

It's hard to believe that it's been over a year since Ash, a dangerous fugitive, kidnapped me from the side of the road, forever intertwining our lives in a twisted dance of fear, desire, and ultimately, love.

Together, we've carved out a life for ourselves in this remote Alaskan wilderness, far away from the chaos and judgment of the outside world. Here, we're free to be ourselves and explore the depths of our passion without fear or shame.

I close my eyes and silently thank the universe for bringing Ash into my life. I know our journey is far from over, but I'm ready for whatever it may bring. I've got Ash by my side, and that's all I need.

* * *

THANK YOU FOR READING *CARJACKED!* Did you enjoy it? If so check out my other books.

More books by me:

Stranded: A Dark Christmas Novella

Welcome to Carnage: A Dark Romance Halloween Novella

Salvation: A Dark Stalker Romance:

ABOUT THE AUTHOR

I've always been drawn to the dark side of fiction. My stories? They're an exploration of that darkness, filled with mysterious masked men, fearless heroines, and spice that'll set your Kindles ablaze.

Ever since I can remember, I've been captivated by the darker side of romance. It's necessary to add I don't condone these kind of relationships in real life. However, the intoxicating chase, the deadly dance, the heart-racing fear, and an irresistible attraction I adore writing.

I exclusively publish on Amazon, providing a thrilling escape for those who dare to venture into the dark side of love and lust. If you've read my book and found yourself wanting more, follow me on Amazon or social media for updates on my next dark novella release. Your adventure is only a page flip away.

f a

ALSO BY THIS AUTHOR

Welcome to Carnage
Stranded
Salvation
Carjacked

Made in United States
Troutdale, OR
07/02/2024

20966829R00137